PRINCE OF

PRIDE

PRINCES OF SIN:
SEVEN DEADLY SINS SERIES

K. ELLE MORRISON

This novel is a work of fiction. All characters and events portrayed
are products of author's imagination and used fictitiously.
Editing by Caroline Acebo
Proofreading by Norma's Nook Proofreading
Cover Designed by Cassie Chapman at Opulent Designs
Interior page design by K. Elle Morrison

Kellemorrison.com

Print ISBN: 979-8-9887063-4-2
Ebook ISBN: 979-8-9887063-3-5

To Nes.
Thank you for being my friend
and inspiration for Nestra.
Ipos is a lucky demon
XOXO

DEAR READERS

This book contains material that may be considered inappropriate for readers under the age of 18.

These materials cover:
Graphic sex between consenting adults. Elements of family dynamic/expectations, CNC,
Depictions of loss.
Elements of religious trauma.

Please leave a review ;)

OTHER TITLES BY K. ELLE MORRISON

Blood On My Name
Audiobook:
Blood On My Name

The Princes of Sin series:
Prince Of Lust
Prince Of Greed
Prince Of Sloth
Prince Of Pride
Prince Of Gluttony
Prince Of Envy
Prince Of Wrath

The Black Banners Series:
Under The Black Banners
Dagger Of Ash & Gold

To stay up-to-date on upcoming titles, bonus material, advanced reader opportunities, and so much more visit Kellemorrison.com to join the newsletter!

For all upcoming projects and updates from K. Elle Morrison please subscribe to the *FREE* Newsletter!

Kellemorrison.com

Linktree

I

IPOS

I'd known the call was coming.

I'd *seen* a prophecy that meant the death of one of his holy brothers, so Lucifer was keen to hear it for himself.

What I hadn't expected was the request that came next.

I stared down at my feet in the chamber outside Lucifer's throne room. The obsidian floors reflected the dread on my face. I had been waiting in the line of lesser spirits for over an hour, and after every slam of Lucifer's door, gut-wrenching screams plagued the hall moments later. Whatever their misdeeds had been against our king, each paid with their blood and soul.

The door opened again, and a strong, gruff voice coughed out, "Ipos, Prince of Pride. Come, brother, and be counted."

Paimon, a king in his own right, was Lucifer's footman. That made him one of the most hated demons to exist. He was also spineless and rarely removed his nose from Lucifer's rectum to breathe fresh air.

I followed him into the deep chamber that held a long table with seventy-one chairs. Each was emblazoned with the name of one of the Fallen, but we were rarely called to sit upon them anymore. Lucifer never sat at the table but lorded over it from his perch, which was where he was waiting for me on his throne made of the skulls of men, beasts, and monsters atop a platform made of gold and carved red crystal.

The doors shut behind me with an unseen force, closing off any exit from the venomous being that sat before me.

I gulped down any fear that Lucifer would be able to scent and squared my shoulders before striding toward him.

The scene put to shame all human lore of the original fallen angel, highest king of demons, Hell, and sin. With his fingers steepled and tapping his scruff-covered chin, he was the epitome of intimidation. Lethal. Cunning. The truest of nightmares. Pure and unmistaken evil. Yet, he held the face of an angel, the grace of the most holy of sons dipped in the most potent of poisons.

I bowed my head and greeted him with honor. "Your Majesty. How may I serve you?"

When I looked up, the edges of his lips curled into a cocky smile. "It would seem that the Prince of Sloth has finally returned from his traipse around Earth. What a heavy burden it must have been on you and your fellow princes."

"There were extenuating circumstances for the abdication of his duties—"

"Do not placate me as if I do not hear everything," he scolded. "Gaap's absence will not be tolerated any longer. And as your punishment for allowing such negligence to occur, you will be tasked with finding something that was stolen from me. A ring."

My spine stiffened at the demand. "A ring?"

"It once hung upon this chain." He tossed the thin gold necklace into my hands. The vibration of holy energy still lingered in the metal.

"You have thirteen days to retrieve what has been stolen or the gates of the Nine Circles will have a new warden." His voice lowered to a deadly resonance. "Don't disappoint me."

2
NESTRA

"Ma! Are you home?"

Of course she was, but my papa's truck wasn't in the driveway, and it looked like my brother's car was missing as well. He was likely still in class. His semesters have been full since he got into his PhD program, and he had his residency at the local clinic.

"Kitchen." Her voice came through the living room over the game show playing on the TV.

I should have known she would be in the kitchen by the volume, and that was where she spent most of her time while I was growing up. If she wasn't helping my brother with school projects or taking communion at the church, she was cooking.

"*Mi corazón.*" She greeted me with a smile and a plate of food. "Take a seat."

I smiled and kissed her cheek, then I took my plate to the table and dug in immediately.

"How was work? Did Mrs. Willis pick up her boswellia for her arthritis?"

"Yes," I said around a mouthful of garnachas, a bit of pickled cabbage falling back onto my plate.

"And . . ."

I rolled my eyes. "And the blessing jar to protect her from her ex-husband."

"That scumbag has been sniffing around again, and the last time he put her in the hospital." She dried her hands on a dish towel before coming to sit with me at the table.

"May the Lord bless her and His grace protect her." She crossed two fingers over her chest and made the sign of the cross before gripping her rosary.

"I could always give her something to put in his tea," I said under my breath, but I still got a swat on the wrist.

"Nestra!" My mother scolded, but she couldn't hide her smile.

"Men like him have always been the problem. They take and take but never have to answer for their crimes."

"It is not up to us—"

"To be righteous, for His hand is mighty," I

finished for her. "Ma, he's a piece of shit who you just expressed hate for."

Her hands went up into the air at my feminine rage. She didn't like to admit it, but she loved that her daughter was so headstrong. When I opened the apothecary three years ago, I'd assumed she would cry for my soul and show up every day to pray me into submission. Turns out, she believed that the herbs and medicine that I provided for our community were holier than anything Big Pharma was pushing. She'd even convinced everyone at church to come to me when they had minor ailments. Ma liked to say that the herbs and compounds I sold were blessed by Jesus and that was why they worked so well. I didn't have the heart to tell her that I prayed to the old gods and studied the craft of heretics.

My papa was always the breadwinner, working as a land surveyor for the state, but my mother was the authority we'd all had to abide by. The first rule was going to Sunday Mass and following the sacraments of the church until we were old enough to make our own decisions. Though my brother was an adult and in medical school, he was required to continue to go to church with our parents every week since he still lived under their roof.

"Mama?" My brother's voice broke the annoyed silence between our mother and me.

"Kitchen," I called back to him.

His tall, lanky frame came through the kitchen door, and I could see he was carrying two backpacks that looked like they weighed more than he did.

"Nes, what are you doing here?"

He dropped his bags then leaned down to kiss our mother's temple before going to the stove to make himself a plate.

I wrinkled my nose at his back. "You didn't miss me, Nico?"

"You'd have to be gone for more than twelve hours for me to miss you, buttface," he said over his shoulder.

"Buttface?" I clutched my imaginary pearls and waited for him to join us at the table. "Is that an official medical term?"

"It is now. I'm going to name the disease after you." He shoved a spoonful of rice into his mouth but couldn't hold back his smile.

"I told you I'd be famous one day," I said to our mother, who was shaking with laughter at our bickering.

"I'm serious," he said without any actual stress in his tone. "You were supposed to have a date tonight. I personally vetted the guy for two weeks before I gave him your number."

Anthony was in Nico's cohort. He wanted to specialize in pediatrics, but he was boring as hell. We'd had two phone conversations and I'd almost fallen asleep during both. He'd gone on and on about the incubation period of chickenpox for almost an hour.

"He canceled," I lied.

"When?" he countered.

"Last minute."

Nico glared at me, likely debating whether he should drop me letting another potential suitor get away. "Nes, I thought you said you were ready to settle down and find someone?"

"She will find the right person when the time is right. There is no rush," Ma chimed in, patting my shoulder.

"Her standards are too high," Nico muttered before taking another large bite.

"As they should be." Ma puffed her chest with pride, bringing a smile to my face.

"Ma! He's the top of our class and on a full-ride swim scholarship." Nico threw his hands up. "He volunteers at homeless shelters and the Humane Society. Last Christmas, he sang a solo at his church's choir and then played one of the wise men in the youth group's Nativity play."

Ma took our arguments in for a moment then turned to me. "You can reschedule, right?"

"Maaaaa!" I hid my face in my hands.

"He sounds like a kind young man, Nestra," she replied. "Give him a chance."

I glowered up at my brother. "You *had* to tell her about the choir solo."

"Stop being so stubborn and I won't have to pull out the big guns." He shrugged.

It wasn't that I didn't want to date or find someone to spend time with. But I was close to thirty and fed up with men's bullshit. Every man I'd ever dated had needed to be taken care of, and I wasn't interested in raising someone's son before possibly raising my own offspring. My mother wanted to be a grandmother so badly that she'd started working at our church's daycare two days a week just to have that fresh baby smell on tap.

My brother wanted to find someone to take care of me, but it was our father who pressed the matter to a different level. In our family, it was important that his daughter find a husband who could contribute to our family as a whole. Not any man would do. My potential husband needed to be resourceful, wealthy, and a strong leader.

My papa had immigrated to the US from Guatemala when he was a small child, and though my grandparents had eventually moved home when he was a young man, he had never been back to Guatemala to visit. He'd gotten his position with the county surveyor's office and climbed the ranks to be head of the whole district. That meant he only took holidays off work.

He'd sent our mother, my brother, and me to meet our extended family once when we were in elementary school. My mother had made the experience memorable, but she swore to never go back again. Apparently, her mother-in-law did not agree with how she was raising her children, and the entire summer they'd bickered behind our backs.

Our mother's family was scattered around the Californian coast. Her parents lived in San Diego, but her sister lived a few miles down the freeway from Palo Alto. Family gatherings with cousins and the church were always filled with questions about when my brother and I would settle down and have families of our own.

Nico didn't face the same pressure as I did since he had entered the world of conventional Western medicine. He was going to be a doctor, which earned him golden boy status among our relatives and friends.

"I wonder if Papa knows anyone at work you could date." Ma took her phone out of her pocket and scrolled through her contacts.

I sighed, defeated by the glare in my mother's eyes. "I'll reschedule."

I knew I wasn't going to win or get dessert if I kept pushing.

3

IPOS

I had a feeling about who was responsible for taking Lucifer's ring, but I had no proof. Coincidentally, my suspect was in close contact with another being that could tell me more about the trinket I was after.

The energy coming from the simple gold chain felt holy. My guess was that Lucifer had had the ring long before the Fall or he'd borrowed it from an angel and had refused to return it. My concern came from not knowing which angel the ring belonged to and what power the ring held. The impact could be detrimental to the human race.

My first stop was The Deacon, a nightclub in Los Angeles owned by the Sitri, Prince of Lust, and his Watcher Angel companion, Ezequiel. During the day, the club was as silent as a monastery, and after the conversation with Lucifer, I took the opportunity to collect myself before confronting my fellow prince upstairs.

As much as I abhorred Sitri's decisions, I had to give him credit for building this empire from the ground up over the last hundred years. He and Ezequiel had their hands in many different pots and had accrued vast human wealth. This establishment catered to a need between demons and the souls of humans. Secret pleasure rooms lined the walls of the downstairs floor, and the newly renovated lounge upstairs was perfect for much more intimate deals between the powers of Hell and human world leaders.

This wasn't the first visit I'd made in the last several months, and I knew he wouldn't be pleased to see me. Still, I had a feeling it wouldn't be my last.

I sat at the bar to wait for Sitri or Ezequiel to find me, but it was their Reaper who gave me a gruff greeting. "Hello?"

I looked over my shoulder and, unimpressed with her meek nature, I turned back around to down the tequila I'd poured.

"Are you looking for Sitri?" she called again, and I ignored her further.

I didn't answer to neutral beings like Reapers. I was here for her prince.

"Listen." Her voice shook now. "I don't know

who you are or why you're here, but unless you start talking, you're going to have to leave."

As she fitfully demanded, I got to my feet and addressed her. "I am Ipos, a prince of Hell."

She stood her ground. "Well, prince of Hell, I am a Reaper, and your status means nothing to me. So, again, either tell me what you are doing here or leave."

Her chest inflated with her declaration. I bit back a snide remark but watched as her spine straightened.

"A Reaper, huh?" I folded my arms over my chest. "What would Sitri need a Reaper for?"

"I'll let him know you had questions for him when you stopped by."

The grin that spread over my face was likely more sinister than I intended, but she held firm nonetheless. She was the first witty Reaper I'd encountered. Beautiful too. It wasn't hard to see why Sitri had formed some sort of bond with her. His scent was all over her skin. Ezequiel's too.

What caught my attention next was the vision that flashed over her eyes: images of a hospital room and a woman in a bed. She was being summoned for a charge right in front of me. I'd never witnessed a Reaper's visions before and hadn't expected to share one with her. But as hers faded, my own came through. I *saw* what would happen if Sitri and Ezequiel were the ones to accompany her.

Scorched earth and high-pitched screams from desolated buildings surrounded the Prince of Lust and the Watcher Angel. Their eyes were pitch-black and their faces covered in the blood of innocents. If they saw their mission through, they would start a war that no being would survive.

My eyelids blinked the empty nightclub back into focus. The young Reaper still stood before me. If I didn't offer my services, she would be the catalyst of Heaven and Hell raining down on this plane.

I cocked my head and cleared my throat.

"I see." I took a few steps around her, waiting for more visions to come to me. "I see much more than you know."

"I don't care what you *see*, demon. Either leave or tell me what you want."

"You have somewhere to be, right?"

My words rendered her speechless.

"I also know you need assistance getting there." I waited for her to work out my abilities for herself before finishing my thought. "And that you can't ask Sitri or Ezequiel this time."

"Why would you want to help me?"

"Because I have *seen* what would happen if you took Sitri and Ezequiel with you, and as another warden of this plane, I can't allow that type of destruction."

I held out my hand for her to take.

The prophecy I foresaw in her eyes was one of wide destruction, and the sooner we stepped through the void and away from the prospective bombs she'd fallen in love with, the better.

Once her purpose was fulfilled, I traveled back through the void to Sitri's front door. He would know she was missing from this plane. The quick glimpse into the connection the Reaper, Sitri, and Ezequiel shared was enough to let me know that her return to the folds between planes would be a hard blow to their world.

I took a deep breath and pounded on the door. A few moments went by with no answer so I knocked again.

"Sitri," I called.

He opened the door and his shoulders sank.

"Ipos," he greeted. "This isn't the best time. I've had my fill of family reunions for the millennium and have my own worries to attend to. So whatever it is you've come to ask for, I am not in the position to grant it."

"I came to speak with Ezequiel," I said, glancing at the broken Watcher sitting at the kitchen island just inside.

"He isn't available either," Sitri answered and took a step over to protect his partner.

"I saw that when I met your Reaper downstairs." I raised my brow to Sitri.

Ezequiel jumped to his feet. "What are you saying? You know where she is?"

"The price of being all-knowing is that I was an intruder in the fate of her third charge. She needed help, and I saw the outcome if the likes of you two had gone with her." I pinged my eyes from one to the other, not wanting to inspire any sort of action. "I did what needed to be done. What you wouldn't have allowed to happen."

Ezequiel looked me over, and the wheels in his mind turned. He must have decided that whatever had transpired between his Reaper and me had been for the good of all and slumped his shoulders.

"Now. I've saved your asses, and in return, I need information about a small copper ring that has gone missing from around Lucifer's neck." I narrowed my eyes at my fellow prince.

"I don't know where it ended up," Sitri answered.

I could feel the remnants of the ring's energy on his fingers, but it had long since found a new owner.

"Fine." I directed my next question to Ezequiel. "What was its purpose?"

"I'm assuming you're asking me because you're assuming it's angelic?" he snarked.

"Something like that." I shrugged. I could feel that it wasn't demonic, but I couldn't be sure that it was holy.

Ezequiel said, "Depending on which of our siblings it belonged to, it could be used to heal wounds, cure illnesses, or even revive those in a deep sleep. Or it could simply be tacky jewelry."

I took in this information and felt out the implications of what it could mean. "Thank you. I'll assume our debts are equal."

"Yes"—Sitri's chin pointed down the hall—"but I also know another debt needs to be settled. Gaap is in room 406."

"Is that so?" The twinge of rage slipped through my words.

"It is." His eyes sparkled with a hint of mischief. "And he's vulnerable. There's a Hunter on his trail."

It was maddening that Gaap had come back to the States and had come to Sitri's door for help. Gaap was in my debt, but Sitri was currently too unstable from matters of the heart to be trusted with as dire a circumstance as a Hunter.

"Good luck, Sitri. I hope you all find what you're looking for," I said before turning down the hall.

I got back in the elevator and rode it down to the fourth floor to the apartment that Sitri had loaned to our most wayward brother. I'd been stupid to accept Gaap's legions and part of his region as my own, but I'd thought I was doing the right thing by giving him a break. During the Fall, Gaap had been one of the most valiant warriors. He'd lost his way over a century ago, but in the last fifty years, he had used his human form to garner fame, fortune, and flocks of human women at his feet.

Those temptations were difficult to resist, but his addictions ran deep. Being Prince of Sloth made him susceptible to every intoxication, including a lover's touch. He'd rarely been seen without his pupils dilated or his arms empty of bodies to use for the night. I knew I was running the risk of walking into an orgy, but as long as he was capable of walking, he'd be useful.

I didn't give him the courtesy of a gentle knock. My fist pounded against the door until the lock clicked and Gaap opened it with vigor.

"For fuck's sake, Eli, you sure have become impatient since I saw you last—"

"Not this time," I said, and the cocky smile melted from his face. "I see you haven't changed a bit. Slacking off while everyone else cleans up your mess."

I stepped past him and over the threshold of the apartment. As predicted, a trail of clothing led toward the bedroom. He wasn't alone, but it would seem that there was only one companion within.

"And you are still tall and intimidating. Neither of us made room for growth, it would seem." He scoffed. "If you're here to demand I take back my legions and territory, I'm a bit preoccupied at the moment. What, with being hunted by a saintly priest and all."

He walked over to a cabinet for a glass, filled it with water, and drank it down without stopping to breathe. I didn't doubt he'd been exerting himself all night. The musky scent of sex and stale liquor on his breath told me as much.

"I came to ask the Watcher a question, but Sitri was eager to let me know that you were here. Sounded like he wanted to get rid of you as soon as he could."

"Can't blame him. I've not been the smartest of us." He shrugged. "And I do tend to leave a mess of the dwellings he loans me."

His lean body was covered in tattoos, and the tight briefs he wore rode up his thighs, revealing dragons, a pentagon, clocks, human skulls, and so many other symbols of his time living out his human desires. I didn't doubt he'd covered the sigil bestowed on him by Lucifer at his crowning.

"That's what you'd like us all to think, isn't it? Prince of Sloth was too dim-witted to see the effects he inflicted on those around him. We both know you're much cleverer than our brothers suspect."

Unlike Sitri, Stolas, or even Orobas, I could *see* his potential. He didn't instill great hunger or thirst in mankind. He inspired apathy toward the Father, but most of all, an apathy toward righteousness— that could free humans from a path of blind devotion. Many of our brothers used their abilities to turn hearts away from goodness for their own gain. But Gaap, if he chose, could turn this plane into something worth saving, unburdening souls of obligation and allowing them to act on free will alone. I believed in my brother, but he would never see it for himself.

"What brings you out of the desert, Prince of Pride?" he demanded.

"Lucifer has sent me to find something that was stolen from him. You wouldn't happen to know anything about an ancient copper ring, would you?"

"Who in their right mind would steal an artifact from the all-powerful Emperor of Hell? And what would make this ring so valuable that he would send the all-knowing seer to look for it?"

I knew why I was sent, but Gaap did not need to know every detail.

"Your guess is as good as mine, but I have a feeling the magic surrounding the ring is hiding it very well. I can't manifest a full vision of its where-abouts, but I know there is a magical signature emit-ting from it. It's faint here in Los Angeles, but it's close."

"How close?" he asked.

"It's in California. It hasn't crossed the desert to the east or the waters to the west." I looked through the folds of time and space once again to *see* what I could of the ring.

"What would someone use this ring for?"

I smiled to myself at his interest. He always did love a good puzzle. "Ezequiel didn't know exactly, but if it was once in the possession of a guardian angel, it could be used for good. Or some semblance of it."

"Lucifer was holding on to a weapon of...good?"

The thought hadn't crossed my mind. If it was a weapon, it might have gone unused for a reason that could be a detriment to Lucifer and, in turn, all demons.

"Whatever it was being used for, it is greatly missed." I ran my fingers through my hair then tied it up.

"Speak what you want from me and be on your

way." His attention snapped to his guest, who must have been stirring. "I have my own interests to attend to."

Annoyed but unsurprised by his lack of focus, I pressed on. "I need you to take a little trip down south. I'm going to go north. I have a small hunch that the Leviathan might know where the ring would be."

The Leviathan had been inhabiting the body of a priest this lifetime, and though he was willing to take my call, I knew he'd be more talkative if he received a visit from a prince in person. Being of His creations but not considered one of the most holy made him eager to be acknowledged by one of us.

"Where is he?"

"San Diego. La Jolla, to be more specific."

"Eligos will be here tonight. I can't leave until he cloaks me."

I paused on this for a moment. Eli had been in utility often as of late, and something about that had me taking note.

I rolled my eyes. "Fine. I'll text you the address."

4
NESTRA

I cut my car's engine in my driveway and took a deep breath. Idly, I spun the copper ring on my finger and sent a prayer to the divine to soothe the tension migraine that had bloomed from staying too long at my parents' house.

My brother hadn't let go of the date that I'd canceled for the rest of the evening. Once my papa got home, Nico told him why I was under scrutiny and, to my surprise, Papa had joined in on the castigation.

When I'd had enough—and called Anthony to reschedule in front of everyone—I got in my car and drove several blocks before blasting Sleep Token and screaming along with the lead singer for catharsis.

My house sat back at the end of my street. The looming forest behind separated the neighborhood from the Santa Cruz Mountains. Tall redwoods, firs, and oak trees sat in thick clusters, and coyotes yipped in the distance as they hunted in the moonlight.

I'd always felt more at peace at night when the world was quiet and I could pretend to be the only person for miles. Aside from a couple other homes on my street, I was alone. Mr. and Mrs. Collards, my elderly neighbors, were a sweet couple that checked in on me a few times a week and dropped off banana bread. It was always fresh and warm. When I'd bring their empty baking dish back, I always brought a few ointments and milk thistle tinctures to help with their arthritis and liver health.

Tonight, the lights inside their home were already dim, but they'd left their porch light on, likely noticing my car wasn't in my driveway and not wanting me to come home in pure darkness.

The night-blooming cereus that hung over my doorway shone bright white and was prime for picking. I'd been cultivating it for years, and though its blooms were hard to catch, the wait was well worth it.

In mystic practices, the cereus flower was significant for rituals. Medically, it was invaluable. Aesthetically, I loved how the underwhelming cactus bloomed during the full moon once a year and shed its flowers a day or so later. It was a test of my patience, and I had been blessed by the spirits with dozens on this night.

With my arms full of the blooms, I fumbled for my keys and unlocked the deadbolt then pushed into the doorway.

An impatient meow greeted me.

"Hello, Lore. Yes, yes. I know you're hungry."

My cat followed me into the kitchen, purring and brushing his large, black body over my calves. Lore had found me about three years ago when he was a scrawny little kitten. I'd come home from work to find him sitting on my doorstep, covered in fleas. After a thorough bath and a trip to the vet, he'd moved right in. For the first year, I expected him to run off, but he never once went beyond my gate. I suspected the table scraps and special wet food were better than catching mice out in the mountains.

I unloaded the flowers then bent down, scooped up my hefty cat, and took him over to the fridge to pull out a snack for both of us. He sniffed at my chin and gave me a prickly lick.

"Here you go," I said, setting him down and scraping the last bit of wet food from a can into his bowl.

I washed my hands, careful to scrub the dingy old ring I'd been wearing for months, and then grabbed a spoon for the pint of ice cream I was taking to the couch.

My phone vibrated as I took it out of my pocket.

ANTHONY

I can't wait to finally meet you tomorrow.

I rolled my eyes.

Nico talked to me about Anthony way too often, so I couldn't imagine what he'd told this man about his witchy, apothecary-owning sister. Nico had also shown me photos of Anthony from his social media. He was good-looking, tall, and fit. He played sports for Stanford, loved to hike, and went to the gym at least once a week, even with his full load of classes and internship. He was superhuman.

NESTRA

I'm looking forward to seeing you too.

I could wait forever to go on a date with a guy who was obviously busy and enjoyed hustling. On the other hand, I enjoyed slow weekends at home. I worked all week in the shop with one part-time employee, and when I was done, a long walk in the woods behind my house was the only recreation I wanted to incorporate into my life. I loved my curves and the strength my body held in my thighs and hips.

The last thing I wanted was some man pushing his ideals of Western medicine body types on me. He could take the BMI scale and shove it right up his ass.

ANTHONY

> You have no idea how long I've been thinking about you. I could hardly concentrate at the gym tonight.

> I was thinking after dinner, you could show me your apothecary? Nico told me that you've been healing people through passion and nature.

Nico didn't say that. He thought the apothecary was my way of rebelling against the medical system, and in a way it was. Big Pharma was bleeding people dry for medications created in a lab. I couldn't cure cancer or any other serious illness, but there were plenty of ailments my herbs and plants could manage without the risky side effects.

For a moment, I thought about showing him my deadly herbs cabinet.

NESTRA

> Maybe another time. Tomorrow is shipment day. It'll be a mess.

A lie.

ANTHONY

Have I secured a second date already?

NESTRA

You haven't even met me yet. You might not want a second date.

ANTHONY

You've had me chasing after you for weeks. If I wasn't interested, I wouldn't have waited around. I know what I want, Nestra. I want a chance to get to know you.

I didn't know if I should cringe or melt at that statement. I liked a commanding attitude, but something wasn't sitting right with his flavor of possessiveness. It felt forced, like he was trying on this attitude for size and it didn't fit the ego he was toting around.

NESTRA

What do you want to know? You get one question for the night.

ANTHONY

Just one?

NESTRA

What will we talk about tomorrow if you ask more than that?

ANTHONY

Fair enough. What is your favorite flower?

I thought about the baskets of night-blooming cereus. It was beautiful and powerful. It symbolized hope and was a potent medicine for the body. I replied to his text with an article about the flower's benefits.

When several minutes passed, I assumed he'd fallen asleep or had lost interest in the conversation. I started an episode of the reality show I was binge-watching and dug into the cinnamon dulce ice cream. Then my phone buzzed again.

ANTHONY

I can see the similarities. Elusive, mystical, rare.

NESTRA

High maintenance.

ANTHONY

Noted. I can't wait to see you tomorrow. Goodnight, Nestra.

NESTRA

See you tomorrow.

I opened the shop like any other day, but that was the normalcy. There was a rush of customers who came in to pick up their orders in the morning, and new customers drifted in and out well through the afternoon. A few blocks away, there was a summer festival blocking the road, so the store received a steady stream of foot traffic.

When Kelly, my part-time assistant, came in for her shift, her jaw dropped at the number of bodies packed into the small space. We sold several dozen remedies, salves, ointments, and candles, and by closing, our tea selection was almost sold out, and the tinctures shelf was bare.

I handed my last customer her bag of creams and candles then waved her off before Kelly locked the door and turned over the "Welcome" sign.

"Holy crap! I would have brought a second energy drink if I knew how crazy today was going to be." She untied her apron and set it on the counter in front of me.

"I would have brought a change of clothes. I don't have time to run home before my date." I checked my phone to find several notifications from Ma, my brother, and Anthony.

ANTHONY

Hope you're having a good day. See you soon.

When I didn't answer, he sent another message a few hours later.

ANTHONY

Not to sound desperate, but I'm really looking forward to seeing you tonight. Don't break my heart, okay?

I let the smile creep up my cheeks.

NESTRA

Work has been busy. I can't wait for the day to be over. See you soon.

"What's that doe-eyed look for?" Kelly sidled up next to me and peeked at the message. "Oh, a boy."

She nudged my shoulder playfully and grabbed her purse from under the counter.

"He seems like a good guy." I sounded less convincing than I should have.

"I bet he's terrible in bed," she said, pulling out her own cell and checking her notifications.

"Kelly!"

"What?" She shrugged and gave me a look of indignation. "It's a fact. Any good dude is terrible in the sack. Remember Josh?"

Josh was her heavily tattooed ex she was obsessed with for over a year before she'd met her current boyfriend.

I gave her an accusatory squint, "I thought you said he never got you off?"

"He didn't, but he was so sexy and did things that Rob would never do. I may not have ever gotten off fully, but every time was earth-shatteringly hot." She rolled her eyes back and opened her mouth wide while fanning herself.

"You're a mess." I shook my head.

"Rob is great. I mean, the man camps out between my legs, but Josh was a whole other devil. Something about those toxic ones."

Her defense was weak, but she wasn't wrong. Every jerk I'd been with had been better than the nice guys. I needed someone who wasn't afraid to throw me around a bit, really sink their teeth in and leave their mark on me to find the next day. By the impression I was getting from Anthony, I wasn't going to be getting what I was craving.

"I guess I'll let you know if we get that far." I looked down at my dress, which was splattered with stains from a jar of salve I'd spilled earlier. "But I feel so gross. I should cancel."

"I think Charlotte's is still open. Come on, I'll go with you."

Charlotte's Boutique was just a block over and one of my favorite places to shop. The owner, Harriet, always had great finds with size inclusivity. I knew I could find something there that I wouldn't wear just once.

"Alright, I'll meet you out front. I have to lock up the tills really quick."

I took both register drawers to my back office and deposited them in the safe. Normally, I would have counted the cash and run it to the bank, but that task would have to wait.

I rummaged through my purse for the jewelry that I'd taken off for demonstrations. The sickening feeling in my stomach subsided when I slid the last piece into place: the little copper ring. I had grown so attached to it after I'd found it in a thrift shop uptown. The ring was old and dinged up, but it fit me as if it had been made just for my finger. Whether it was fate or magic, every bit of witchcraft I attempted while wearing it felt more solid. I could feel energy hum through me during rituals, as if to say I was not alone.

It had come into my life at just the right time. I'd hit a financial bump in the road—too many medical bills after a car accident—and Ma had been sick. The ring had caused a tenfold increase in the power of the spells I'd cast and the medicine I'd made.

Since then, I'd been using the confidence the ring gave me to heal my customers. I felt like a conduit for something more powerful than myself, but it was almost too hard to explain where the power came from. The shop was more successful now than it'd ever been, and my mother was as fit as a fiddle. It was a gift from the divine that allowed me to help those who needed it most.

I said a quick blessing and ran out to meet Kelly to find the perfect outfit for my date.

5

IPOS

I'd followed the energy signature of the ring all the way up to Palo Alto, but the witch community was much bigger than I expected. The hotel I checked into was downtown near Stanford University. I knew it was close but couldn't pinpoint the location without help. An hour after I settled in, Gaap and his companion showed up at my door. Gaap had sent me a text before driving up, saying that he hadn't been able to finish the task I'd given him but he had something else that Duke Eligos said would suffice.

I paced the floor. "The Leviathan didn't tell you what he'd intended to give to you?"

Gaap and Pru sat at the foot of the king-sized bed and watched me closely.

"He didn't get the chance." Gaap sighed with the

weight of his guilt for the loss of the great beast on his shoulders "Eli sent me with this." He held out a rolled-up piece of paper tied with velvety black hair. "Eli said this spell should help you find the ring." He scooped Pru into his side, and she laid her hand on his thigh.

"What did you have to give him in exchange? Eligos never gives favors without strings."

"What's another debt to owe?" Gaap shrugged but smiled. "Now that I've done my duty, I reclaim my legions from your command and will enforce my crown with a worthy partner at my side."

The glint from a large diamond on Pru's finger caught my attention. The gold band held an inscription likely put there by Haniel the Alchemist. It was meant to bond part of Gaap's being to her. I supposed there was no reason he couldn't claim her soul and bestow a portion of his power onto her. It was likely for her protection more than anything, but the gesture would send a message to both Fallen and Holy that Pru was untouchable.

"I'm proud of you, brother." I reached out my hand to him, and he stood and took it.

The moment our skin touched, a vision flashed over my eyes of their future together. I pulled him into my shoulder and allowed what I had *seen* to flow through my body into his.

Quick images flashed of Pru standing at his side

at a commitment ceremony, then glimpses of the travels they would have, and, finally, a moment they would share that not even I should have been privy to. He pulled away, and his watery blue eyes filled with gratitude and understanding.

Most of my premonitions held death, destruction, and pain. Hope was rarely a message I could deliver, and giving it to one of my brothers was sacred—and rare.

"Thank you, Ipos." Gaap squeezed my shoulder. "For everything."

Pru was not just a new adornment to my brother's crown. She was his equal in spirit and fire. I'd never experienced that sort of love myself. There had been lovers through the years, both human and demon alike, but none had felt like my match.

For the first time in a long time, I was envious of one of my brothers, that he had found someone who complimented him, but more than that, someone worth truly living for.

Gaap wrapped an arm around his soon-to-be bride and kissed her temple, and she grinned up at him.

"Time for our next adventure." Gaap turned to lead her out of the hotel but paused at the door. "Call me when you're finished with this assignment. We have catching up to do."

I nodded, and he shut the door behind him.

The sun would be going down in a matter of hours, and I would have to search for the ring's trail on foot. I looked down at the slip of paper in my hand. My thumb brushed over the lock of hair that bound it. Fragments of wherever Eli had gotten the hair still clung to it and radiated from my fingers to my wrist. It was evil, vile, and holy.

I paced the floor for several minutes, weighing my options. There was no telling what the spell would hold or what price would be demanded if I used it. Magic was an unpredictable element of the universe that was rarely free from consequences. Without any other answer, I sighed and pulled the loop of strands off then tucked them into my pocket.

The yellow paper was stiff from too many years of holding its secrets. The etchings were barely visible when the paper unfurled to reveal an ancient language long since forgotten. I rolled my tongue over the syllables, and the air around me hummed with the magical trace. Invisible to my eye, it wound around my fingers, up my arms to my shoulders and chest, then down my torso all the way to my feet. My nerve receptors came alive in the spell's wake.

With renewed purpose, I made my way out of my hotel room and down to the lobby. I knew where to go and what the witch would feel like when I saw them. The spell had been crafted to find the being who possessed the ring and had locked on their soul's essence. I broke into a jog when my feet met the pavement outside.

6
NESTRA

Anthony was waiting for me outside the restaurant when I finally arrived. I was twenty minutes late, and though he smiled when he saw me, there was annoyance in his voice when he greeted the waitress with a gruff, "Is it still happy hour?"

I'd found a cute strapless dress that flowed down to my ankles, but the shoe selection had taken longer than it should have. The strappy beach sandals complemented the purple flowers on the black, silky fabric, and the wedge heel kept the hem from dragging on the ground.

"I was starting to worry that you were going to stand me up," Anthony said as the waitress poured our water.

"Sorry. I swear, I've been thinking about seeing

you all day. It was just so crazy at the shop." Under the table, I spun the battered ring on my thumb and focused on the nicks and gashes I'd memorized during long sessions at my computer. Silently, I prayed it would loosen the knots in my stomach like it did when I was filling out tax documents.

He gave me a dazzling smile while tracing the rim of his cup with his finger. "You look beautiful."

Maybe he was nervous?

"You too." The words tumbled out, and I internally cringed.

He huffed a laugh then looked at the menu in front of him. In my defense, he did look beautiful. His hair was teased and moussed to perfection, and his light-blue dress shirt accented his broad, muscular shoulders. As far as beauty standards went, he checked many boxes: tall, well dressed, chiseled jaw, perfectly sparkling smile that could melt glass. Even his brown eyes had depth and shades of amber. He was wearing a fair amount of clothing but it was obvious that he spent a lot of time and energy at the gym.

"The artichoke and goat cheese appetizer looks good. And the arancini. Want to get both and split them?"

"That sounds great." I'd been staring too long and hadn't even glanced at my own menu. I looked over to the bar and saw the bathroom hidden back in the far corner. "I need to freshen up. Feel free to order them while I go to the restroom."

I didn't give him a chance to answer. I needed a little bit of liquid courage if I was going to be able to continue sitting across from this man. Dating gave me stress hives normally, but my nerves were amplified on a setup like this. Anthony was attractive, but he was also someone my brother saw every day and would likely be friends with after they graduated. If this date went south, I could very well hear about it for the next twenty years.

At the end of the bar, there was a scruffy-looking man with his red hair tied up in a bun and sunspread freckles over every inch of his exposed skin. He sipped on a beer and watched me approach but didn't say anything when I stopped and wedged myself at the lone stool between him and a group of guys watching a basketball game on someone's phone.

I waved down the bartender, who came right over.

"What can I get for you, hun?" She leaned against the bar and waited for my order.

"A shot of tequila and a lime wedge, please." I pulled out my wallet and slapped down a ten-dollar bill.

She gave me an impressed expression.

"Just one?" the well-tanned mammoth of a man said, his voice just as gritty as he looked.

"Have to start the party somewhere," I said, sounding all too much like Papa.

The bartender returned with a bottle, a shot glass, and a small bowl of limes.

"Two more." The stranger tapped a couple of his long fingers on the bar in front of him and smiled.

The bartender blushed, clearly affected by the breathtaking smile, but she topped off two new glasses and slid them between his waiting hands. He held one up to me, brought it to his lips, but then waited for me to mimic him.

"Alright." I picked up my shot glass and took the burning liquor down in one motion.

Though his eyes twinkled with the humor of the moment, he only gave away a cool grin as he opened his lips and welcomed the alcohol with a tip of his head.

I bit into a lime wedge, and the segment burst and covered my taste buds before I could scowl at the bitter notes. He plucked a slice and took it between his perfect teeth to scrape the inner fruit out then deposited the rind in the empty glass.

"Here." He nudged the last shot closer to me. "You didn't give me a chance to buy the first one."

"Oh…" I looked over to Anthony, who was taping his thumbs on his phone. "I'm actually on a date."

"I know." The golden scruff on his face caught the light as he smiled. Full and devious. "You looked nervous. Consider it a gesture of luck."

I spun the ring on my thumb, and his eyes cut to it for a long moment before they locked with mine again.

"I usually make my own luck." I smiled to myself and twisted the glass around in my hand, debating whether to accept his offer.

"You don't need it," he returned with a curious cock of his head.

"Yeah, you're right. He's a nice guy. I'm just being silly." I felt like I was defending Anthony to this stranger.

"Sure, if that's the sort of guy you're into."

"What's that supposed to mean? You don't think I'm into him?"

"No, I don't think you want a nice guy. I think you want someone who will challenge you."

Shocked and stunned, I struggled to form words. "I haven't known him long enough to know that he wouldn't challenge me."

"Maybe not, but I can tell." He smirked, his eyes not leaving mine.

"Oh really?"

"Absolutely." He waited for me to verbalize the obvious curiosity on my face, but I stayed quiet. "He sat across the room and watched as I bought his date her second drink of the night."

My blood ran cold. He had to be bluffing.

I glanced over my shoulder, but Anthony was still staring at his phone. When I turned back around to a smug grin, I shoved his shoulder and laughed with him.

"That was mean." I finally took the shot in my hand then bit into the last lime.

"It was, but the look on your face was worth the bad karma."

Whether he saw it as a way to one-up another guy or if he actually was hitting on me, the butterflies in my stomach fluttered all the same. This man had hubris seeping from every pore. It was the type of confidence you would expect from frat boys who knew how to go down on a woman.

"If he does disappoint you, I'll be here for a bit," he said, raising his half-empty beer glass.

I suppressed a smile and the itch in my spine to abandon my date for the mysterious stranger who'd made me laugh within moments of meeting.

I stepped back from the bar, hoping the distance would give me the strength to leave. "Thanks for the drink."

I turned and walked back to my seat across from safe, handsome Anthony.

My new mission of the night was to not, under any circumstances, glance at the gorgeous man at the bar.

7
IPOS

I'd found her in a small clothing shop across town, then I followed her to the hole-in-the-wall bar and grill. When she sat down with the prim-and-proper-looking human, I'd laughed to myself. He was smitten with her instantly, but her reluctance felt more complex. I had a hard time getting any sort of read on her soul—it could have been the cleansing and protection rituals she'd performed on herself—but the emotions on her face were as clear as sunlight.

The would-be doctor tried for the fourth time to reach across the table to her. I *saw* his future as a successful pediatric surgeon, his large future practice, and the wife he would eventually have several children with. But she wasn't the woman he was currently pursuing.

When their check came, the future doctor paid

and left a large cash tip. He got to his feet and stood next to his chair awkwardly as the witch gathered her things. She had restrained herself from looking for me, but her curiosity finally won out when her date placed his hand on her back to lead them outside. Her eyes locked on mine with a mix of uncertainty and a cry for help.

I had planned to follow her home, sneak into her house, and retrieve the ring while she slept, but that was no longer an option. I stepped in front of them when they reached the door and blocked the only exit.

"Excuse us," said her date.

"You're welcome to leave," I responded, "but she's staying with me."

She shot me a look then watched her date for his next move.

"What the fuck is your problem?" He slipped his arm out from behind the witch and crossed both over his chest.

"A very many things, but at this moment, you're trying to leave with my girl." I grinned and stepped into him, cutting her off from his side.

She moved behind me unnoticed.

"We're just trying to leave. Whatever you're doing isn't funny. Come on, Nestra, let's go." He reached a hand behind him to find her gone. "Nestra?"

His command was as frail as the spine he was pretending to possess. He'd never been in a physical altercation. From what I could *see*, all his arguments had been with the woman he'd dated over the years, and the idea of having to defend someone terrified him.

Nestra, the little witch, shook her head. "It's fine, Anthony. I'll call you later."

"Wait. Do you know this guy?" Anthony's face twisted into disgust.

"We're old drinking buddies," I chimed in with a cockier smile.

Anthony looked from me to Nestra then back. His confusion marred his face with deep lines on his forehead and I could swear I saw a vein in his temple ready to burst.

"This is ridiculous. Nestra. Tell this guy to fuck off and come back to my place. Like we planned."

That was why she had sent a silent call for help. She didn't know how to tell him she didn't want to go home with him. Something about the situation either felt threatening or like a trap, and human men often didn't understand the word *no*.

"In case you didn't hear me before, she's staying with me." This time, I allowed my voice to deepen and didn't hide the demonic resonance underneath.

His shoulders shuddered, and I'd be lying if I said it didn't encourage me to push him further. I wanted to humiliate him, leave a lasting impression on his ego, but with Nestra's trust hanging in the balance, I took a step back.

I leaned down to Nestra's ear. "Order us a couple more shots. I'll be right there."

Her brown eyes met mine as I pulled away, and the grateful glimmer in them snagged at my breath.

What was it about this woman's careful gaze that made me weak in the knees?

She nodded and weaved through the growing crowd to the bar. The fabric of her dress clung to her thick curves, and I watched her hips sway. The promise of tequila and her full attention on me was enough to make my mouth water.

"I bet you're pretty proud of yourself," Anthony said, his head shaking.

He would never comprehend how true his statement was. I gave an agreeable shrug and made to step around him when his arm flung out to block my chest.

"Are you going to fight for her honor?" I taunted. The challenging smirk on my face turned his red.

His breathing picked up and the tendons of my hands tightened, and my eyes narrowed in on his soft jaw.

"You'd like that, would you?" he pressed. "You want to hit me and show her how much more of a man you are than me."

I wasn't a man. I was the beast that hunted men in their darkest nightmares.

My influence was the reward for living a life of pure self-indulgence. Boastful gluttony could build a man up just to be torn apart by those who envied and hated him. And standing at the cusp of Anthony's demise was sending an itch down my arms to my fists.

"I don't have anything to prove," I answered. "But if you'd like to see how I finish a fight, you're more than welcome to start one."

The sweat on his brow beaded into a stream down his cheek. When he finally gave in to his level head, he stormed out of the restaurant, careful not to knock his shoulder into me on his way. A few patrons laughed off the show and went back to their meals with a fresh discussion topic for their evening.

Nestra was sitting at the end of the bar with four shots of tequila and a bowl of limes. She typed out a message and sent it off before putting her phone face down then releasing a heavy sigh.

"That bad?" I said, sitting on the stool next to her and downing one of the shots.

She knocked one back, shivering as the liquor hit her palate, then licked her lips before answering. Her nose wrinkled at the last bitter notes as she reached for the salt shaker and lime. "I'm sorry." She sucked hard on her lime wedge. "I panicked when he suggested we go back to his place and I didn't have a reason to say no."

"You don't need a reason."

"I know, but I had every reason to say yes." Her watery eyes finally met mine. "He's smart, handsome, courteous, and my family approves of him."

"Naturally, that last part makes him repulsive." I wrinkled my nose in disgust.

Her sweet laugh broke my mocking expression into a smile. Her warmth was contagious. The lines near the corners of her eyes said she laughed often, as opposed to the sun-stricken lines of my face. I often went years between sightings of other beings in my secluded patch of desert. I preferred to be far from intrusive *visions* brought on by visitors or trespassers. But a longing I hadn't expected crept into my bones when she looked at me like I'd validated her instincts.

"He may as well have been an alien lizard man from a far-off galaxy with how much my brother adores him. I'd actually canceled on Anthony before and I couldn't put my finger on why the idea had bothered me so much until I realized that no matter the outcome of tonight, I wasn't going to feel good about myself in the morning."

"What do you mean?" I nudged a shot closer to her hand then took the last one in my fingers.

"If I'd gone home with him and it went further, I

would have felt gross. But if I would have said no then never called him again, I would have felt like I'd let my family down or proven them right."

She knocked back the alcohol then tore into another lime.

"Disappointing family is a universal experience."

I knew that all too well. Our Father had never forgiven those of us who'd deviated from his grand plan. In every glimpse of the ever-changing future I'd *seen*, we would never be reunited by His choice.

"They're all I have."

The sadness in her voice brought me out of my own family drama.

"You could have anything you want," I assured her, but the magic of the ring made it impossible for me to *see*.

"I have everything I need. I own my home. My business is thriving and growing. I'm helping people heal, and I have the opportunity to learn and practice my craft every day."

"Sounds busy. Doesn't that get a bit lonely?" I was prying, but the more she trusted me, the easier it would be to slip the ring from her finger at the end of the night.

She sat with the question for a moment before she answered, "Yes. Don't we all get lonely, though?"

I shrugged and she went on. "We all want someone to come home to and feel balanced with.

Someone to take the stress off your mind and hold you when the bad days win. I don't want much, but having a partner would be . . . "

She looked dreamy-eyed, but I could see the sadness lurking beneath. The worry that she would never find that sort of companionship or vulnerability with someone.

Being alone wasn't the worst fate, but feeling empty was.

I cleared my throat, and she brought herself back from the consuming darkness.

"It also helps if they're good in bed." I winked.

"Oh Goddess, yes!" She burst into laughter. "It's been months since I've gotten laid." The pink in her cheeks deepened into a new shade of red and her eyes widened in shock for what had come from her own mouth. "I shouldn't have said that to a total stranger." Her hands shielded her blushing face.

I looked around us. "What strangers? We're old drinking buddies, remember?"

At that moment, I wished we were the only ones left in the restaurant. The heat on her skin made my cock twitch to life, and I had to shift to hide the evidence.

"Fuck, that's right." She shook her head. "If I haven't said it yet, thank you—I just realized that I don't even know your name."

"I'm Poe, and it was no problem."

"I don't know what I would have done without you. You really saved me tonight," she said sincerely.

"Maybe I had ulterior motives," I said, the underlying truth masked by a playful lilt.

"You are a man. I'd be surprised if you didn't have ulterior motives in everything you do."

"Whisking beautiful women away from their dates sends a thrill through my spine like no other."

Another dash of crimson flashed over her cheeks. This time, her thighs clenched, and I wanted nothing more than to get on my knees and spread them open to taste the excitement I'd inspired.

"I actually believe you." She tucked her hands between her knees. "This is just any old Thursday night for you?"

I turned my chair to cage her between my knees then slid my arm across the bar in front of her. I leaned in closer. Her perfume mixed with the alcohol on our breath and the musk of my cologne. I could have watched her take in our mingling scents for hours.

"Not a single woman here compares to you. The moment you walked in, I knew I had to have you all to myself. It was pure luck that you decided to let me keep you company."

She melted into herself, and her lips parted without words on her tongue. I ran a finger up her arm, over her goose bumps, to her chin. She didn't pull away as I tilted my head and brought her face closer to mine. I left room for her to change her mind, but after another still moment, I pressed a soft kiss to her full lips.

She held her breath then let it out slowly when I pulled away for our eyes to meet again.

"That was nice." Her voice was hushed and airy.

"Can I kiss you again?"

She gave me a gentle nod but closed the distance between us herself. Her lips parted over mine, and her tongue teased until I deepened our kiss. Her hand braced on my thigh and moved closer to my cock when she searched for more contact with my body.

I wrapped an arm around her back and pulled her into me until she was on the edge of her stool, forcing her to use me to keep upright. A satisfied hum vibrated over her tongue and my core filled with need. I fought the urge to pin her to the bar and rut into her until she was coming and screaming my name.

My restraint thinned the longer she allowed me to touch her. I had to regain perspective and remember what had brought me here to my hands full of her soft and bountiful hips. Permitting myself only two more seconds of weakness, I bargained for a third, then a fourth. But when the air in my lungs was thick and I was forgetting why I needed to let go, she pulled away. Her soft gaze made the situation in my pants close to dire. The look of drunken pleasure on her features could bring me to my knees.

She let out a heavy breath and fanned her face before she said, "Those shots really went to my head."

We relieved each other with shyer smiles then relaxed back into casual conversation for another hour until she was sure she was sober enough to drive herself home. I walked her out to her car and waited until she drove out of the parking lot before getting into my rental and following her by several car lengths. If I let her get too far ahead, it would take days that I didn't have to find her again.

She'd kept her distance when we'd said our goodbye but threw her hands around my shoulders when I'd offered my hand for her to shake. That was when I felt the burn of the ring's magic on my skin. The sting of its rejection had left a charred hole in my T-shirt.

She would have to surrender the ring willingly or I'd have to find a way to contain the thing to transport it to Lucifer. That was a hitch I would have to deal with when I found my way into the witch's house.

After almost an hour of driving to the outskirts of the city, she finally parked in a driveway but didn't get out of her car. I lurked in the shadows, but she seemed to be on her phone so I snuck around the back of her house and found the door right outside the kitchen.

With a quick wave of my hand, the deadbolt slid over. The clicks of the pins in the last lock gave me entrance to the house. A shunted yellow path of light from the neighbor's porch came through her living room window. I sat on the armchair in the corner and waited for her to come inside. She had protection spells invoked everywhere. The fact that I'd been able to cross over the threshold of her door proved that our time together had deemed me a friend in her eyes. The purring cat who jumped into my lap also viewed me as worthy.

I knew she would be frightened when she found me in her sitting room, but I had no ill will or intent to do her harm. Only time would tell if that intention remained true.

As I took in her cozy home, I battled the memory of her luscious curves between my thighs and the sound of her heart racing at my slightest touch. Our kiss had woken something within me that refused to subside. For a moment, I let myself imagine a world where she and I would have come back here together. But that fantasy was fleeting and vanished entirely when she unlocked the door.

8

NESTRA

My brother texted me back while I was at the bar with Poe, but I had waited until I was in my driveway to reply. My phone rang immediately after I'd sent off my text.

"You ditched him for another guy?" Nico's voice thrashed against my eardrum.

I held my phone away from my face, but I could still hear Nico cursing through a long lecture on respecting people's time and feelings.

"How could you do this, Nes! Did you even know that other guy, or did you rope him into your self-destructive behavior?"

I took a deep breath to restrain the hot tears filling my eyes. "Anthony wasn't for me. I'm sure he'll find someone else next week."

"No, he won't," Nico barked back. "He really

liked you and you embarrassed him in front of a restaurant full of strangers. He's scarred for life."

"Then maybe he needs to grow a spine. I didn't want to go home with him then have to hear your judgment tomorrow. No matter what, my actions would have gotten me yelled at."

The emotions were too much to hold back any longer. My hoarse voice encouraged the river of tears that slid down my face.

Nico may have been my younger brother, but he was one of the men in our family. He and my father were supposed to protect and care for me, but that often meant arguments like this. He thought he knew what was best for me, but he also wanted me to be someone else's responsibility. If I ever married, my spouse would be given the duty, and Nico could live his life however he chose without familial guilt.

"I—"

"Good night, Nico. I'll talk to you tomorrow."

I hung up then turned my phone to silent. Nothing he said would make the experience any better. My head was aching, and my chest burned from alcohol from earlier.

I had successfully pushed the dirty thoughts about Poe out of my brain for what seemed like hours. His body on mine had felt so good. From his broad, solid chest, and his thick, muscled arms to his soft lips, everything about him was surreal.

Fuck. Why hadn't I gotten his number?

I looked down at the notifications on my phone and saw three missed calls and a dozen texts from my brother. If I had let anything more happen between Poe and me, Nico and our parents would have ruined what probably would have been one of the best nights of my life.

My fingers had brushed over the front of his jeans and felt the beast he had been containing in them. I had gotten him hard with just a kiss, and that sort of power filled my ego as much as my stomach with nervous energy.

I let myself relive that too-brief moment once more before I shook him from my head, gathering my purse to make my way to my front door. Poe would forever be the one that got away—and inspiration for many vibrator-induced orgasms. Which sounded like the perfect way to end such a roller-coaster of a night.

Walking up the steps to the house, I waved at Mr. Collards's shadow in his kitchen window. He waved back and turned off the bright floodlight on the side of his house as I pushed the door open.

I didn't bother flicking on any of my own lights once inside. My goal was to prepare myself for bed by brushing my teeth and removing all my clothes before slipping between my sheets. Then I'd reach into my side table drawer and grab ol' faithful, a rabbit-style toy that had never once left me unsatis-fied. Tomorrow would be another busy day with many regulars picking up their orders for the week-end. My well-earned mental breakdown would have to wait one more day.

Several steps into the living room, I realized that Lore wasn't there to greet me with his hungry meows.

"Lore," I called out in the dark.

"Here, kitty, kitty." The dark, deep voice came from behind me.

Ice plunged into my gut and my spine went straight. A second later, a lamp in the living room sparked to life, and my throat tightened around a strangled scream for help. It was Poe. In my house?

"W-what are you doing here?" I managed. "How did you get in?"

His light eyes locked on mine while his fingers moved over the small lump of fur in his lap. Lore purred loudly.

I warred with every instinct in my body.

Running from him would be useless. Even if I got through my front door before he could slam it shut, he'd catch me before I got to my car or the neighbors' house. The other option was to try the back door but it led out to the woods. I knew those paths better than he could ever, but judging by his physique, he would catch me within seconds.

I couldn't fight him off; he was at least a foot taller than I was and built like a muscular tank. The bulge of his arms had made me weak in the knees before, but now all I could picture was them flexing as he strangled me.

"I know what you are, little witch." His voice sent goose bumps over my skin. "You have something that doesn't belong to you, and I need it back."

He picked up my cat and got to his feet slowly. Lore struggled in his hands then jumped down to the couch before running off to my bedroom, likely to hide. The coward.

"Take whatever you want, just please don't kill me." I took a step back, but two of mine was one of his and he was quickly towering over me.

He considered me for a moment. "Anything I want?"

Fuck.

"I can think of many things I want from you." His eyes heated and dropped to my lips.

My lungs strained for more air as something squirmed low in my belly. I took another step back, but his hand clamped around my wrist.

"Your pulse is racing, but you're not scared." He smiled wickedly, and the bloom of excitement in my core swelled. "I could make your heart beat faster and your voice hoarse from screaming."

"Please stop," I croaked.

"What do you really want me to stop, little witch?" His hand smoothed up my arm and settled at the nape of my neck. He pulled me closer. "Is that what your heart is screaming to me?"

His thumb at my jaw tilted my face up to his. His nose brushed mine, and his tongue swept lightly over my lips.

I fought through the panting breaths I was taking. "Just tell me what you came for. I'll give it to you. Then you can leave."

He leaned away enough for our eyes to focus on one another. His long, blond lashes hung low over his bright-blue irises, and I could have watched him look at me like that for eternity. No one had ever gazed at me with such hunger. I wasn't sure if he wanted to swallow me whole or wrap his hands around my throat.

A small voice in the back of my head hoped that he would do both.

"I came for this." He held up my hand with the battered copper ring. "But I'm having a hard time not demanding more."

Why would he want the ring?

"Take it," I urged.

"You're going to make it that easy for me?" He cocked his head, and a shimmer of something white flashed around his irises. "I was hoping you'd put up a little bit of a fight."

His hand loosened as he stepped away. A predatory grin spread across his face, and my thighs clenched to silence the thrill that he'd inspired between them.

"We both know I wouldn't win."

"I'll give you a ten-second head start. But if I catch you, I take anything I want from you."

My heart hammered in my chest and my pussy ached. The muscles in my legs tightened as blood pumped faster to my limbs.

"You want me to run?" I stepped back and the carpet of the living room gave way to the tile in the kitchen.

"Does that excite you? Do you want me to hunt you down amongst the trees and show you the monster you lured in?"

I did.

I didn't know why I wanted him to chase me. Or why I wasn't terrified of what would happen when he caught me. Because, let's face it, he would catch me no matter how much time he gave me.

"What if you don't find me?"

That look in his eyes said I was his prize and he had no intention of losing this game. "I wouldn't disappoint you like that." My innards turned to mush. "One. Two."

I didn't wait for him to get to three.

I dropped everything and ran to the back door.

As fast as my feet would carry me, I bolted into the tree line and weaved back and forth around the thick oak trees. The long skirt of my dress caught in my sandals, so when I thought it was safe to stop for a moment, I gathered up the hem into a thick knot then kept running. I cursed my choice of shoes, but I couldn't take them off. Stones and thorny weeds would slow me down far more than the wedges.

The trails I'd taken hundreds of times were foreign to me with so much adrenaline pumping through my veins. Each turn on the path led me farther from my house but into more worrisome territory.

My muscles were on fire, but I had to keep going. I couldn't give up so easily, and the thrill of what would happen if he caught me pushed new energy into my limbs.

A snap of a branch under a heavy footstep caught my attention, and I paused at the split of the trailhead. The sound was close. Far too close to be him already. I didn't know how long I'd been running, but I could still see the roof of my house through the clearing. The longer I stood still, the louder my pulse got. He would catch up if I didn't pick a direction.

Without thinking, I turned and zigzagged between the two worn trails until the space between them became too separated by bushes and trees. I took the path going north, where the trees thickened and would give me more shelter to hide. If I were lucky, my footprints would be hidden by the bundles of pine needles that littered the underbrush.

The denser the trees became, the darker the ground grew under my feet. I stumbled half a dozen times before I reached a large boulder. I crouched down at its base to rest and tighten the straps of my shoes.

"I'm getting closer, little witch." Poe's voice came from somewhere deep in the woods. "Can you feel me?"

Not that I could explain how or why, but I could feel him closing in on me.

My eyes darted around, looking for his ginger hair, but the branches above were tightly woven. He would have to step carelessly through beams of moonlight peeking through the bare spots to give away his location. So instead of waiting to see him, I decided to make him show himself.

A few palm-sized rocks were scattered at my feet. I picked up the darkest one and tossed it into the trees far from me and heard a thud as it hit something solid then rolled on the ground.

His footfalls grew louder, and my pulse pounded.

"You're very clever," he said with a low chuckle, "but if you want to see me, you're going to have to come out from where you're hiding."

The cat-and-mouse game was coming to an end, but I was going to fight him the entire way to the finish line.

"If you catch me, you have to tell me what you want the ring for." I tried my best to not sound out of breath, but I was sure he could tell I was exhausted and cornered. "Deal?"

His throaty laugh came before his answer, his voice much closer than before. "You want to strike a deal with a demon?"

"Yes." The muscles in my legs coiled, ready to lunge in my last attempt to avoid him. "Promise?"

"I promise."

I choked on a scream as he materialized behind me. His rust-colored hair had come loose from the tie, the soft waves draped down to the top of his bare muscular shoulders. I dodged his grabbing hands and dove between him and the boulder trapping me in place. My feet scrambled under me, and I finally got the rest of my body upright to run, but he was hot on my heels.

The thick trunks of trees passed by in an almost solid wall but by the pool of light coming from the moon, there was another clearing about five yards ahead. I swallowed down as much air as my lungs would take and pushed myself harder.

Closer and closer to the bright spotlight on the dried grass.

It felt like the end to the madness, but as the tips of my toes reached it, his arm banded around my waist. He hauled me back against him in an astounding move, and we landed on the ground. My stomach dropped and dirt and sand stirred up into my nose, eyes, and mouth as I screamed. The echo around us didn't sound like a call for help; it sounded like excitement.

"You're all mine now, little witch." His gruff voice in my ear cut off all oxygen from my brain. "Finders keepers."

"Fuck!" I kicked and flailed but didn't make contact.

"I intend to," he said, and the distinct sound of a zipper being pulled made my heart skip a beat.

He grabbed a handful of my hair and pulled me up to his chest. My exposed skin was damp and the hair on his chest rubbed over my shoulder blades.

His free hand ripped the thin material of my dress, and it fell away as if it were made of nothing more than tissue. He took a firm hold of my breast and pinched my nipple between his knuckles, causing me to call out once again.

"You can be as loud as you want to. There isn't a soul for miles that will hear you coming around my cock." His hot breath on my ear contrasted with the chilly air, making my skin come alive.

I folded into him as his other hand moved from

my breast to my panties. I knew he would find me weeping for his touch. I whined when his fingers dipped inside me with little resistance, and he groaned in return.

"Can you feel what chasing you has done to me?"

He pushed his jeans lower, and his hard cock pressed to my ass. Only the thin fabric of my panties separated us, but not for long. His thick length slipped up to the small of my back, and I realized just how large he was. The man was massive. Much bigger than I had thought by the brief touch at the bar.

"Please." My throat was still strung tight from his fist in my hair.

What was I asking for? The clawing need in my chest would eat me alive without release. But the nagging voice in the back of my head told me that I should feel shame or reluctance for giving in to the man who'd broken into my house and was about to fuck me after chasing me through the night.

A growl from his chest silenced the last echo of my hesitation. In one clean rip, his hand left me completely naked with my knees bruised and covered in dirt. I sucked in a shallow breath as he gripped my hip to pull me into him. The head of his cock pushed inside, spreading me until I didn't think I could handle anymore.

"That's right," he gritted out through his clenched teeth. "Beg for my cock to fill this tight pussy."

His head dropped to the sensitive flesh at the nape of my neck, and I hissed his name as he bit into my shoulder. Holding me in place with his teeth, his hips gave a pulsating thrust and he sank deeper inside of me until I was bursting. Every slow and deliberate movement of his hips built the pressure in my core until I thought I couldn't take any more.

He finally let go of my hair to nestle his palm under my chin and his fingers wrapped around the column of my neck.

He released his jaw, the spot aching from the pressure already. I moaned in frustration and relief. "I can't. Please. I need to come."

His fingers circled my clit and he bucked behind me.

"I am what you need." His raspy voice demanded control. "I will challenge you. Hunt you down. And fuck you senseless like no man could."

My core tightened at his strained voice. I was so close to climax, and the ragged sound of desperation in my ear was going to make my body erupt.

"Don't stop," I cried. "Don't fucking stop."

"Nothing could stop me from fucking what's mine. I'm going to use this pussy until you're raw and dripping with my cum."

He slammed into me, the tension in my core mounting with every rough thrust. His hand around my throat tightened until I could feel my pulse in my temples. He wasn't trying to hurt me, but the increased tension sent my senses into overdrive.

"Oh fuck, Nestra." My name on his lips sent a wave of electricity through me. "I'm going to mark your body and soul so every being knows who you belong to."

Every word sounded like a struggle to keep his composure, but he strummed his rhythm until I was crashing around him. The swears and curses strung between calling out his name echoed into the night air.

His cock throbbed with the constricting pulses of my pussy until we both were panting. I melted away from his hold and down onto all fours to catch my breath. He rested his head on my back, and the cascade of his long hair fanned over my skin. After-shocks of electricity shot through my jelly-filled arms and legs, into my fingers and toes.

Before I could compile a full thought, he was on his feet, zipped up his jeans, and wrapped me up in my discarded dress to gather me in his arms.

I closed my eyes and nuzzled into his chest, which smelled like damp earth, amber, and sweat. The strap of my left sandal had snapped, so walking back to my house was going to be tricky. I lifted my head to express my concern for our trek back, but his lips captured mine. I wrapped my arms around his neck and felt a strange vacuum sensation around us. And as if the moon had been extinguished, we were plunged into darkness.

9
IPOS

With Nestra's spent body cradled in my arms, I took us through the void and reappeared in her living room. Her cat greeted us with a bellowing meow.

"I need to feed him," she said, looking over her shoulder.

We watched the black cat's tail swish into the kitchen. Then, I set her down on her feet and steadied her.

"Where's your shower?"

She hummed and pointed to the first bedroom door.

"Feed your little familiar." I held her face in my hands and kissed her brow. "Then come find me."

Her jaw dropped, and I could feel her eyes on me as I made my way to her bedroom. Her large bed was piled with pillows. Above it was a tapestry with the phases of the moon, and soft fairy lights lit the ceiling. Just left of the bed was the door to the bathroom. Though the rest of her house was a direct reflection of her personal style, her shower was spotless. Every item had a place and the sterile, precise angle of her hair tools and toothbrush piqued my curiosity.

I pulled back the shower curtain to find several bottles and tubs of various scrubs, cleansers, and soaps aligned on a caddy. Each carried a scent I'd noted on her skin: lavender, rose, jasmine, and sage. The complexity of the combo had made her easy to track. Nothing out in those woods smelled so sweet.

I turned the shower on and let the water warm. Not knowing her preferred temperature, I let it run on the hottest setting and let the steam fill the room.

"The beast is satisfied." She came from behind me, clutching a towel around her body.

I raised a brow at her, and her cheeks heated.

"I meant my cat, Lore." She relaxed her shoulders when I huffed a laugh and took the corner of her fluffy towel between my thumb and forefinger and mulled it over for a moment. "My dress was a goner. Not a great loss, but I've learned my lesson when it comes to running in wedges."

My shirt was lost to the night, but by the look on her face, she didn't mind the view.

"I like this look on you." I pulled her into my

arms, and the feel of her skin on mine sent blood straight to my cock.

"Do you want to tell me before or after we shower about the ring?" she asked, holding up her dust-covered hand.

"After."

I wasn't ready to move past the afterglow or redirect my thoughts to the reason why I'd intervened during her night out. I kicked off my shoes and socks then removed my pants. We stepped into the shower together and I pulled the curtain closed, taking an extra moment crowding her under the shower's stream.

The water flowed through her dark hair and over the curves and dips of her frame, washing away the evidence of our fun in the dirt. Her knees were bruised and scraped, but the sight only made me harder.

Chasing her in the dim light of the moon had freed a part of my soul that had been buried for too long. The thirst that only the taste of a woman could quench. The hunger for flesh between my teeth and the calls of pleasure caused by my hands and cock. An obsession that I'd repressed was bubbling to the surface and Nestra was its focus.

The small cuts I'd sustained while running after her stung, but what caught my eye were the burns the ring had left behind from her fingers clawing at my arm while I fucked her.

"How much do you really want to know?" I ignored the searing marks on my skin and watched as she washed the last stain of me from between her legs.

"Everything," she said with confidence. "You said you were a monster. That I was striking a deal with a demon."

She waited for me to deny my statement while I stalked her. When my silence confirmed her suspicions, I expected her to scream or try to fight me off. But she didn't yield to any other emotion except curiosity.

"You were telling me the truth. You aren't human."

"No, I'm not human. My name is Ipos. A noble prince of Hell and the embodiment of sinful pride."

Her lips parted as she surveyed me. "You're . . . a prince?"

"Of the demonic variety."

She was quiet for a moment and then started to laugh. Her hands domed over her nose and mouth, and her face turned pink.

"You're fucking with me," she finally said through tears brought on by her giggle fit.

"Not at the moment, but I'm contemplating it."

That remark was enough to bring her senses

back. "You're a royal demon from Hell? And you just chased me through the woods behind my house—"

"Then had my way with you." I gave her a cocky smile.

"But why?"

I took a step into her, pressing her to the wall of the small shower. With my hands on either side of her head, I leaned down so our faces were level.

"Because I'm conceited, demanding, and arrogant enough to take what I want when I see it. Your first unknowing mistake was being put into my path. No matter how your date with that asshole had ended, it would have been my cock inside of you tonight."

She squirmed under my gaze, and the need to claim her all over again started to fill my chest and cock.

"Are you always so direct?"

"I don't have any reason to beat around the bush and have limited time."

"What do you mean?"

I reached behind my back and turned the water off. "The ring you have on belongs to Lucifer. I've been sent to retrieve it."

I reached over to our towels and wrapped one around my waist. After stepping out of the tub, I offered to wrap her up in the other. She came to stand next to me, and while I wiped away the beads of water from her skin with the fluffy towel, she looked down at the ring with fascination and fear.

"This is the Devil's ring?" she whispered.

"Technically speaking, no."

Her eyes shot to mine. A wave of relief—or possibly sickness—washed over her face.

"He borrowed it several thousand years ago and it just recently went missing." I tried my best to reduce the situation for her. As long as she gave me the ring, she wouldn't be harmed.

"I have to be dreaming." She walked to her bedroom and sat on the edge of her bed.

I followed and stood over her like an apparition.

She covered her face and took several heavy breaths through her fingers. "The healing I've done while wearing it . . . has been tainted?"

Her hands fell to her lap, and she looked up at me with tears hanging from her lashes. I had no way of knowing if there was truth in her concerns. I got to my knees before her and held her hands in mine, careful to not make contact with the ring.

"Little witch." I lowered my voice and held her gaze. "You have performed great magic before and will do so after the ring is rendered back to where it came."

Her pupils dilated, eating up the rich brown of her eyes as she took me in.

A stipulation of the use of the ring was that the

user had to be pure of heart. I had no doubt that Nestra, who was looking at me so deeply, was nothing but pure care and love. Whoever had bestowed the ring on her had done so either to destroy her goodwill or to amplify the work she'd been doing.

Either way, my task was the same.

"I thought it was making me more powerful, but I figured it was just a manifestation." She pulled her hands out of mine and wiped the tears from her cheeks.

"Only a truly powerful individual could harness its power, Nestra. Don't for a moment minimize your strength to mere belief in an object. You are magic."

The corners of her lips twitched into a smile. I rose to kiss her brow, but her chin lifted for our lips to meet. Her arms wrapped around my neck and the hunger for her returned in an instant.

I scooped an arm under her ass, bringing her to the center of the bed, then pulled my towel off. Hers had already fallen away and her skin warmed mine. My cock slipped over the round of her belly then dipped down to her wet center.

"Ipos." My true name on her tongue was a song. "Slow."

An impatient sound rumbled through my vocal cords, but there would be time for me to ravage her through the night.

"You're making demands now?"

I smiled around her bottom lip between my teeth. This woman could ask me to crawl through a bed of burning coals and I would gladly oblige if it meant I could kiss, suck, and fuck her again. I pulsed my cock at her entrance, teasing at the need I knew brewed inside of her. She tensed beneath me, and her hands in my damp hair stilled.

"Please."

Another groan rattled my chest as I pulled my hips back in concession. I dipped my chin to her chest to take a stiff nipple into my mouth. She sucked in a breath as my tongue curled around the hard nub. Her hips started to grind against my belly, so I gave her the pressure she was seeking by pressing my weight down onto her. I cupped her other breast, sucking and flicking at her nipples until she was soaking my stomach.

When I angled my head up to watch her face contorted in pleasure, I caught sight of something propped in the open drawer of her nightstand. The wicked smile on my face didn't prepare her for what I had in mind.

I got to my knees between her legs, took the vibrator from its drawer, and turned it on. She watched each move in wonder.

"So wet for me." I growled and slipped it between the lips of her glistening pussy.

Nestra cursed and squirmed in my hold, but I tightened my fingers on her thigh to hold her in place. I pushed the head of my cock inside and could feel the needy pulsating of her walls. I was going to show her what slow agony I could inflict until she was begging to be fucked properly.

Her hips rose and dropped, grinding for more friction, but what she craved was depth. A quick, shallow thrust then pulling out completely rewarded me with a frustrated whine. Her brown eyes bulged when she saw the boastful smile on my face.

I circled the vibrator widely around her clit, just missing the swollen nerves and causing her more delicious distress. When I edged inside once more, I pressed the tip of the toy just above the pleasure point. She arched and hissed through the teeth she'd sunk into her bottom lip.

"I could fill this pussy, if you let me. Come on, pretty little witch, let me fuck my pussy." I pushed another inch and waited for my answer.

"Your pussy?" She was breathless, but her sass lingered under her tone.

I moved my free hand down over her clit and circled my thumb over it slowly, adding pressure that made her gasp. I sucked in a breath and pulled my hips back to leave her wanton.

"Isn't it? Look how badly it needs my cock." I

thrust in slower. "Oh fuck. So tight. This pussy was made for me."

Her thighs clenched and eyes rolled as I filled her to the hilt. I bent down to her ear, the pressure of my body and the vibrator on her clit bringing her right to the tip of an orgasm. But it was the shaking moan of my own that pushed her over the edge.

She clawed into my back, and her screams of pleasure turned to pleas for more. I angled my hips and unleashed punishing blows. I let the toy fall away then fucked her hard and rough for making me wait for what was mine. When she crashed around me again, I sat up and retrieved my vibrating teammate to hold over her throbbing clit again. Her fingers dug into my forearms, hanging on to me for dear life when another orgasm wrecked her remaining senses.

"Oh Goddess. Please."

Her words broke and legs shook.

"My cum is going to mark you from the inside out." I grunted, my balls tightening. "Because you belong to me."

"Yes!" she cried out. "I'm yours."

I wanted to watch her take control of her own pleasure. I pulled the toy away and let it fall to the ground, lifeless. Together, we rolled over and I pulled her on top of me. She sank onto my cock with a sharp inhale. The depth my cock reached with her firmly seated felt tight, but when my hands gripped her ass, she started to grind her hips.

Her hands planted on my chest, her nails raking over my skin and digging in to label me as hers. She groaned as the pressure built between her legs again. My cocked throbbed as I got closer to my own release. Her head fell back as she worked herself up into an orgasm that sent goose bumps over her skin.

"That's my good little witch. Come for me." My fingers dimpled her flesh as I pulled her harder down onto me. "You're so pretty when you fuck me."

With her raspy, spent moans ringing in my ears, I spilled inside her and experienced pure ecstasy once again. My cock jerked against her spasming walls, and every nerve buzzed with pleasure and belonging. I was made for this woman. Her body was created to withstand my strength, and her soul would house my immortal one for eternity. I knew it the moment she kissed me, but being inside her set my chest on fire.

She lay down next to me, and we panted in unison. Our bodies were slick with sweat, and the faint light from the window set her skin aglow. True beauty came with vulnerability and comfort and I felt grateful that she was willing to share this quiet, naked moment with me.

She looked over at me with large brown eyes that felt as if they truly saw what I was without fear or hesitation. I kissed her forehead, relishing in the taste of her skin after enjoying me so thoroughly.

We were both exhausted, but my cock was still stiff. I could spend hours inside of her and it wouldn't be long enough. Soon, she would be accustomed to that longevity, but for now, I slipped my hand down and massaged the mess I'd made over her swollen sex.

I brought two soaked fingers to her parted lips and stroked them over her tongue. She licked and sucked on them until my cock jerked. When they were clean, I pulled my hand away with a satisfying pop from her lips. Her tongue traced over her lips, searching for more. I sucked at the tip to take a taste for myself. The lingering sweetness from where we had joined wasn't potent enough to stave off my hunger.

I got to my knees, and pulled her into the middle of the bed. Her legs parted for me easily and she watched me nestled between her damp thighs. Our eyes locked as my hands spread her wet pussy open and I dragged my tongue over her overworked clit. Her body jerked at the oversensitivity but didn't pull away when I went back for more.

She groaned as I lapped up every last drop I'd left behind. My time was running out before I had to return the ring to Lucifer, and I was going to savor it fully.

10
NESTRA

When you're single and self-sufficient for long enough, it takes more than the bare minimum that most people were willing to give to impress you to the point of wanting more. The craving that erupted somewhere deep in my core when Ipos touched me or looked at me was enough to drive me mad.

Ipos consumed me thoroughly—body and mind.

We spent hours worshiping each other. His stamina rivaled my own, which meant round after round of mind-blowing sex well into late morning.

When we finally fell asleep tangled up in each other's limbs, it was the sound of his heart beating that gave me the comfort to doze off. He was real, not a mythical creature I'd dreamed up to soothe my loneliness or carnal hunger.

I twirled a loose lock of his rust-colored hair, which was fanned out over my silk pillows. He was gorgeous. As heavenly as his origin and just as devastating.

How could a man so beautiful be sin incarnate?

I refused to believe it.

He had said earlier that I was made for him. He owned me in the only way I would allow. The whirl of feelings threatening to burst through my chest shouldn't have existed for someone I'd just met. Admittedly, I'd never believed in love at first sight, but what about first fuck?

I shoved those questions away and settled my head into the crook of his shoulder, the notch perfectly sculpted to support my neck. He smelled like desert rain and night-blooming cereus. Of course he did. The demon would hide behind the scent of pure rejuvenation.

His chin grazed over the top of my head and his fingers at my hip tightened as if he subconsciously needed to ensure I was still with him. My heart ached at his content, humming exhale. The imprac- tical urge to climb his body just to feel more of his skin on mine pushed to the forefront of my horny thoughts, but the soreness between my legs stifled the idea to bargain for more rest.

The moment my eyes closed, a pounding from

my living room jolted us out of our postcoital stupors.

"Nestra!" a muffled voice called. "Answer the door."

"Fuck." I scrambled out of bed and put on a baggy T-shirt. "It's my brother."

I searched for some pants and hopped through the bedroom door while pulling them over my ass. A blur of red hair and freckled white skin passed me.

"Ipos, wait——" I reached out to him, but it was too late.

"Who the fuck are you?" My brother's anger rang through my house.

"Someone who hates being woken up," Ipos shot back.

"Where is my sister?" Nico asked.

"Busy."

Ipos' clipped responses were beginning to sound more like threats the longer he stood between us.

"Nestra," Nico called around the large man blocking my front door, his black hair bobbing between the gaps of Ipos' body.

"It's okay." I put a hand on the demon's shoulder, and he peered down at me for a long moment before deciding to move away.

"Who the fuck is that?" Nico's face was red and twisted up in confusion.

"What do you want, Nico?" I ignored the question he likely deserved the answer to.

"Your phone has been off for hours. You haven't called Ma, and you didn't open the shop." He rattled off his list of concerns on his fingers. "You can't just disappear and expect everyone to be okay with it."

My cheeks blushed with shame. I'd all but forgotten I had a real life outside of my bedroom. I didn't know where my phone had gone or what time it was. All I knew was that I was just as angry at being interrupted as I was embarrassed to have been caught slacking on my adult duties.

"Nestra." Ipos pressed into my side, and I realized he was still naked.

My whole face burned, and laughter bubbled up into a fit that I couldn't contain. Both Ipos and Nico watched me giggle, my hand over my mouth, until I was wheezing.

"Go put on some clothes," I coughed out to Ipos, who cocked his head but willingly retreated to my bedroom.

"Nico. I'll call you later." I wiped the wetness from the corners of my eyes. "Tell Ma… Tell her not to worry and I'll be over later tonight."

"I'm not just going to leave." He was fuming at my dismissal, but I was a grown woman and could make my own choices, no matter how depraved they seemed at the moment.

"I have to get ready for work. Like you said, I'm late." I closed the door on a stunned Nico and went looking for the other angry man in my proximity.

Ipos was pulling up his tattered, mud-caked jeans over his bare ass.

"Nico was just worried. He's not usually so—"

"Foolishly indignant?" His words were dry and depressingly human toned.

"Sure."

His mood had shifted, and I wondered if it was because of the complications that came with the intricacies of mortal families combined with the clearing of the haze from our lust-filled night. The sour taste of reality was knotting in my throat. I loathed this feeling and wanted nothing more than to lie back in bed like the visit from Nico hadn't broken through the cloud we'd been floating on. My only other option was to leave and save the dignity I had left.

"I have to get to work." I pulled open my closet doors and grabbed a comfy, flowy dress.

"No. You don't." His body crowded behind me, blocking the rest of the room from my field of view.

I turned around to find him glowering down at me. Tears pricked behind my eyes and I fought back the urge to cry out my frustrations.

"Yes, I do. I have to open up the doors and deliver medicine to my customers. My mother is coming by for a large pick-up order for her church group. And I'm sure she has plenty to say about me ditching Anthony last night. It's better to just get it over with."

He moved in another step. The hangers in my closet creaked as my back pressed into the clothes hanging on them.

"I came for the ring." He held out his hand, his fingertips just under my chin. I set my hand on top and waited for him to take it off of me. "And the witch who wields it."

My heart plummeted into my stomach. He couldn't be serious.

"You said you only needed the ring back." My voice shook.

"The ring will not allow me to possess it. It has attached itself to you, which means you either come with me or you wait for Lucifer to come and retrieve it himself."

A shiver ran down my spine at the latter option. My muscles twitched, but last night had proved that I wouldn't be able to outrun a demon. He would catch me and drag me to Hell, kicking and screaming. I took a shallow breath, my lungs aching to scream.

Ipos' eyes focused on me, and the shadow of his brow erased the kind, sexy man I'd spent the night with. Left behind was the beast who was ready to tear me to pieces.

"Now, now, mighty prince." A sharp voice rang through the thick air. "Who taught you to play with your prey like that?"

II
IPOS

"**I** could ask you the same question, Hahajah," I said to the angel. Her grating presence filled the room with sickening holy light, but she wasn't alone. Vepar chuckled next to her, snide and unbothered. "I believe that's one of Sitri's dukes. Since when do you play with another being's toys?"

"We had a common goal," Vepar said. "Sitri's unhappiness is hard to manipulate alone."

I didn't bother to ask why they were both hoping to destroy Sitri's life on Earth. There had been so many shots fired over the years that grudges ran deep.

The last I'd seen Vepar, he had come to disturb me at my home. It would seem he had moved on from his previous problems and had found new ones to engage in. Hahajah, or Haja, was Sitri's constraining angel. Her appearance proved a theory I had about the ring's disappearance.

All the pieces of the puzzle were falling into place, but the both of them being here together still had mysteries to be told.

"Nestra, darling." Haja leaned over to get a better look at Nestra, who was concealed with the bulk of my body.

I pushed Nestra farther behind me. Her hand gripped my shoulder, and her fingers dug into my skin in warranted fear.

"The ring was yours," I said to Haja, breaking her focus from Nestra and directing it back to the matter at hand.

"It was once." Her manic smile pulled at the dimples in her cheeks. "It'd been tucked away in Hell for centuries. It hardly recognized me when I finally got it back. But it took to this lovely witch with no hesitation. Cheeky little thing."

Haja's sickly sweet tone spoke to how deranged she was, driven mad with her own vanity and being worshiped by humans who didn't know any better. She draped herself on Vepar's arm, and he looked down at her with admiration.

The longer I took them both in, the more I wanted to rip them to pieces for the string of asinine events they put into motion. Screwing with the threads of fate was beyond what I thought either was capable of. My relationship with Vepar was similar to the one I shared with other dukes I'd encountered after the Fall: Vepar reported directly to Sitri, but we sat at the same table in Hell when Lucifer called upon his most trusted soldiers.

Cooperation. That would be a fair definition to describe our relationship. But if Vepar took a step toward Nestra, I would tear him apart without reservation.

"You have thirty seconds to explain why you're intruding on my assignment," I said, voice stern.

Nestra's hold on my arm tightened.

"We're only here to warn you." Vepar held his hands up in defense. "And possibly persuade you to not return the ring."

I shot a look at Haja. "You want the ring back?"

"No, I gave it to this witch for good reason. She has a gift for healing and a purpose that has not been *seen*." Haja twisted her fingers in the air, whimsy returning to her face.

"You gave this to me?" Nestra stepped forward and gazed upon the angel who'd given her the precious gift that had brought me into her life.

"My darling witch." Haja reached a hand out to Nestra but pulled it back to her chest when I gruffed out a sound of warning. "You are meant for great things and this ring will ensure your journey is long and fruitful. I've come to warn you that if you give it back to Lucifer, you will not make it out of Hell to see the future you are destined for."

I circled my hand around Nestra's wrist and brought her into my side. "What is that supposed to mean?"

"You were right, love." Vepar's face brightened with his intrigue. "His *sight* doesn't work around her."

"Not while she wears my gift, sweet duke," Haja answered, but her eyes didn't leave Nestra.

"That will be remedied in a matter of moments," I replied. "Lucifer requires the ring be returned to his possession and has instructed mine to be the hands that retrieve it."

"If you take the ring from her, she will die from the many ailments she's cured while wearing it." Haja's eyes shifted to mine. "You wouldn't want that, would you, Prince of Pride?"

Fuck.

"I hope you're rethinking the hostility you've greeted us with." Vepar smirked. "You can consider the favor I owed now paid."

"If you'd like to save our witch from His Most Dark and Loathsome Highness," Haja explained, "then you need to hide her away."

Nestra turned and looked up at me for an answer, or maybe an explanation.

I took in what Haja said for a moment, but

Lucifer would find us and carry out the punishment he'd promised—and much worse—if I crossed him.

"That isn't an option." I tore my gaze away from Nestra's and looked back at the two guests. "I'm repaying my own debt to Lucifer."

"I'm surprised by your apathy, Ipos," Vepar said. "The smell of sex is still thick in the air. I would have thought you'd want to keep your new friend alive."

"Bite your tongue, Vep," Haja scolded. "Have faith in your prince."

Vepar cupped the nape of Haja's neck and brought her head back to kiss her. Whatever was going on between them was steeped in mutual hate, but being in existence as long as we had been, there were rarely significant reasons for pairings like theirs.

"Please, Ipos." Tears flowed down Nestra's face. "Don't do this."

Her voice was tight from fear and the hope that had been dangled in front of her so briefly, only to be snatched away. Lucifer would send hordes of lesser spirits after her if I didn't deliver the ring, and even if I were with her, I couldn't protect her. She would have to plead her case at Lucifer's feet and hope for mercy, though neither of us had anything to offer him in exchange.

"What Hahajah has failed to understand in cursing you with that ring, Nestra, is the lengths that Lucifer will go to ensure it finds its way back to him."

I turned my back on the troublesome pair so that Nestra's focus was fully on me. "I will do everything I can to bring you home safely. But Haja's proposed plan will not do anything but cause you more harm."

Nestra studied my expression. "You promise?"

I cupped her cheek and pulled her closer so only she could hear me. "I wouldn't disappoint you like that."

A tear trailed down her cheek to her lips, which widened into the first smile I'd seen since we were disturbed.

12
NESTRA

The demon and angel left without any other explanations or a goodbye. I had a feeling that Ipos was more dangerous to them than they had let on.

Ipos instructed me to get dressed in something I felt powerful and beautiful in. Then he would take me to see the Emperor of Hell.

If I were being honest, I felt like a fraud. Hahajah said she'd chosen me because I had a role to play in the future, though her details on that prediction had been sparse.

I didn't want to be part of some grand plan for either the holy or damned. That was never my place, no matter what I chose to believe in or not. But like most things I'd learned in my craft, it wasn't up to me. The powers at be would guide me, and I had to hold on to that faith.

After dressing and fixing myself to feel like a badass witch who was given the power of the universe on my finger, I walked out of my bathroom. Looking around, I wondered if it was the last time I'd ever see the cozy home I'd created for myself.

A sharp pain stitched in my chest at the thought of my family searching for me for decades with no answers. Ma would blame herself, and my heart broke for her. The last words Nico and I shared had been in anger, and part of me hated him for that. I should have stood up for myself sooner and I wished that I'd hugged my brother instead of fought with him.

I worried for Papa and how his health would decline if I wasn't around to supply his teas and herbals. They said people died soon after losing a child or a spouse because their souls couldn't exist without them. Would his heart give out after losing me?

Lore purred and rubbed against my leg. I picked him up and held him close, feeling the vibration from his contentment against my hollow chest. Ipos watched me from the doorway, giving me a moment to dwell in the silent farewell I was giving to my human existence.

"If I don't come back, will you take care of Lore?" I asked, my throat thick with tears.

His features hardened and he gave me a slight dip of his chin as my answer.

I kissed the top of Lore's head, set him on the ground, and watched his tail flick from side to side as he walked past Ipos.

Ipos reached out a hand then waited for me to take it. I took a deep breath, held my head high, and grasped on to him. He pulled me into his chest and fiercely kissed me, stealing the last bit of oxygen from my lungs.

The abyss swallowed us whole. Wind roared around us. Then, my feet hit solid, smooth ground.

"This way." Ipos pulled away and began walking down what looked like an endless hallway.

Each door we passed blurred in and out of focus. The engraved symbols on each seemed to move as my eyes struggled to track them, trying to make any sort of sense of the deep etchings. After passing several, I reached out a hand to feel for proof they were real, but a large hand circled my wrist and yanked me away.

"Touch nothing. Say nothing." His gruff voice thudded against the unnaturally shiny floor.

I opened my mouth, but he shook his head in warning.

"Eyes on me." He stepped closer. "No soul but mine wants you to leave this place, not even your own."

I expected to not understand what he meant, but as if the answer had been a basic math problem, my brain formed the perfect analogy: my soul yearned for a final destination—whether Heaven or Hell, it didn't matter.

There was a sense of peace, not belonging, to the air. Like visiting a dream you'd had hundreds of times. The haze of the grand hallway was empty and vast while being contained and familiar. I couldn't see the ceiling or either end of the hall, but I knew where to go next.

We walked for several minutes before coming to a large carved door with a depiction of a dragon being cast out of the clouds by winged bodies. It gleamed with jewels, gold, and black stone. It was morbid but beautiful. I wondered if it was a celebration or a reminder of the war the Fallen had supposedly lost.

Ipos stood in front of me, and a seam cracked open wider and wider to allow us inside. The chamber beyond held a long table with gaudy chairs surrounding it. I couldn't hide the wrinkle of my nose at all the strange names emblazoned on what I realized were small thrones when we passed one with Ipos' name on it.

At the end was a platform with a few short steps up to a man sitting on a throne fit for his status. He was painfully stunning: a head full of bright blond curls, cheekbones that could cut glass, and full, pouty lips. His blue irises were so piercing blue through the dark tapestries and decor, I would have sworn they were glass.

There was no mistaking that this was Lucifer, God's most beautiful angel who'd fallen from Heaven for his own vanity and greed. The lore surrounding him had inspired men to do unspeakable things. And he was staring at me.

Ice and liquid fire warred in my veins under the weight of his gaze. My feet had stopped just before the first step, and out of panic more than respect, I bowed my head. When I looked up, I was met with a subtle smile that could have easily melted my panties if I had remembered to wear any.

"My liege"—a high-pitched voice came from somewhere around me but my eyes refused to tear away from Lucifer's—"the prince has brought the witch who stole from you."

I shook my head and mouthed the word *no* over and over, my tongue sticky against the roof of my mouth.

"Hush, Paimon." Lucifer's clear voice bombarded my senses. "This mortal has not wronged me. Your thirst for blood and flesh is tiresome."

He cast a lazy gaze to the man off to his side, then to the mountain standing beside me.

119

"You've done well, Prince Ipos. I am grateful for your haste." Lucifer's tone softened while praising Ipos, and a need in my core sparked to life to hear him praise me.

"Sire, this witch possesses the ring and has rendered its power." Ipos pressed his hand to my lower back. "It performed great healing magic for her, and I believe it could do much more."

"Which is why I sent you after it." Lucifer's cutting tone lashed out. "Though you weren't supposed to bring the hand it was attached to."

"Ipos," I whispered under my breath.

Ipos' eyes flared at the sound of my voice, and his lips thinned into a line. I'd broken his rule.

"You told her your true name?" An amused smile spread over Lucifer's cunning features. "How interesting."

"I believe we should try to remove the ring and restore her to her life before the ring fell into her lap."

Lucifer stared at Ipos for what felt like a lifetime. When he got to his feet, he hopped from the edge of the platform to the step in front of me and Ipos.

"Sit down, little prince," he said, fusing over Ipos' long locks, which were draped over his shoulder. "What is your name, witch?"

I looked up to Ipos, who turned his gaze away

from mine. It wasn't a clear answer for permission to speak, so I decided on my own. "Nestra."

Lucifer gave a silent command to Paimon, and a chair materialized at the foot of the large throne. Ipos took a step toward it, but Lucifer cleared his throat.

"For the witch." Lucifer smiled and laid a hand on the empty chair's armrest.

Ipos looked down at me and gave me a subtle nod. His hand at my back moved to my waist, and I relished the warmth of his touch. The gentle squeeze of his fingers released the heavy weight on my chest. He wasn't going to leave me, and the brief moment our eyes met held a promise that he was ready to burn down Hell to keep me safe.

With a deep breath, I ascended the steps to sit in the seat Lucifer had requested. A thick pillow hugged my rear end. It was more comfortable than I expected. Even under the Emperor of Hell's eyes, I settled into the cushion and had no trouble holding my head high.

Lucifer had smiled when I stopped wiggling and held out his hand. Our knees weren't touching, but I hardly had to move to place my hand in his.

His thumb brushed over the ring he'd once owned. "My neck bore this ring for millennia." His voice was thick with his memory, and though I couldn't explain it, the ring on my finger hummed at his soft stroking. "I borrowed it from a lesser angel. She'd promised it would protect someone very dear to me for the rest of time, but it could not protect her from me."

"What do you mean?" I whispered, allowing him to rotate my hand up so my palm was exposed to him.

"Much too long ago, my equal sat at my side. But I was ruthless and cold. Scorned from the battle of the Fall and restless as I pieced together what you see around us."

My eyes followed his hand that showcased the extravagant hall. I'd heard the story of the war between good and evil in Sunday school growing up, but I'd never believed it. It felt too simple and clean. A valiant effort by angels to weed out the vile and envious in their ranks.

For the sake of children and the simple minds of the flock, it was an easy concept to follow: those who lived peaceful and pure lives would live amongst the angels and the Father, and the wicked would be cast out of paradise and into the clutches of the Devil and his minions to be tortured for eternity.

But the demons had their own side of the story. They were once just as holy as Michael and Raphael. Their removal from Heaven was always told as a cautionary tale to blindly obey the will of the Father. To question the All-Mighty was punishable by corruption of your soul.

Though mankind was the spark that led to the inferno of their downfall, demons didn't use their influence over sin to destroy us. They left us to our own devices and watched through our horrific history as we killed each other in the name of men with far too much power.

"I gave my queen this ring to keep her mortal body and soul at my side for the rest of time." Lucifer's voice softened. "But not long after she left me, she saw the cruelty of your plane and felt a calling to heal it. You have the same calling, don't you?"

I nodded and swallowed. The ring around my finger warmed to the rhythm of his thumb over its battered surface.

Lucifer's eyes fell to my neck, and his tongue wet his bottom lip. "She could have been more potent with the ring's help, as you've seen yourself. But she didn't want me to be able to find her. She fled, and it was many centuries before I felt her soul near mine again."

He trailed off, the misty glimmer of his lost love fading into more pain and longing. Who would have known that thousands of years couldn't lessen the sting of a broken heart?

"I'm sorry," I croaked, and I meant it.

To my surprise, Lucifer's lips tipped into a constrained smile. He looked back down at the ring on my hand and sighed. "I kept this token around my neck, allowing it to sear my flesh and remind me constantly of what came from my foolishness. The Fall was minor in comparison to the loss of my darling Lilith."

Lilith. Of course it had been the wife who'd disobeyed Adam and had run from the Garden of Eden. I'd heard the folklore and the variations of her mythos. I knew witches who prayed to the mother of demons for blessings.

"How long will I have after you take the ring back? I just want to say goodbye to my family." I fought the sting of tears in my throat, hoping a show of strength would implore him to allow me to see my parents and brother one last time.

"Your Highness." Lucifer and I snapped our attention to where Ipos stood at the bottom of the steps. "I'd like to offer my services at the gates in exchange for this witch's life. I will personally take responsibility for her existence and split my time between being warden of the Nine Gates and ensuring the ring and its gifts remain hidden."

"A martyr to the bitter end, Prince of Pride." Lucifer gave a low, humorless laugh. "My most noble soldier. I should have known you would fall on your sword if given the chance."

The ache in my chest was chorused by my lungs screaming for air as I held my breath for Lucifer's answer.

Ipos did not flinch at Lucifer's offhanded words and went on with his proposal to get me out of Hell. "Every century, I will relocate the witch. My post will only be empty for as long as it takes me to settle her into a new life."

The details of Ipos' plan sent a new pang of distress through me. I would only see him once every hundred years. He was giving up everything he held on Earth to ensure I could live. But not just live. I would be given immortality and the ability to heal humanity like Lucifer's once-great love had wanted.

How could I possibly repay him for that sort of sacrifice and gift?

If Lucifer agreed, I supposed I would have a hundred years to come up with something.

Lucifer steepled his fingers. The subtle tapping of their points to his chin matched the pulse in my ears.

"For this witch, you'll join me in Hell," Lucifer clarified.

Ipos nodded.

"And leave her on Earth defenseless?" This time, Lucifer sounded confused and offended by the notion.

"Your Highness—"

"I won't hear your thin excuses." The rise in Lucifer's voice caused me to cower in my seat. "She will be an agent of this kingdom, armed with a weapon of heavenly devastation. Her gift would alter the course of His will, and you would not protect her?"

My heart lifted, but I fought the tears of relief pricking my eyes. I looked back at Ipos, whose mouth was agape.

"Speak," Lucifer demanded.

"I won't leave her side," Ipos declared.

Lucifer stood, obstructing my vision, and walked down the steps to Ipos. "I'll take her hair from your pocket."

He held out his hand expectantly, and Ipos' eyes darted between me and the Emperor of Hell.

"Her . . . Lilith." Ipos took it from the front pocket of his jeans and held it up to look at it as if for the first time.

Lucifer plucked the dark lock from Ipos' palm then took out a gold chain from his own pocket. He wrapped the hair around the delicate gold loops and tied it into a knot before putting the necklace around his neck again and hiding it beneath his shirt. A look of relief ghosted across his face as he placed his hand over the new lump.

"Reminders of your past are more important than you think," Lucifer said to the room, the aim vague. "When I held her close, I had everything. I was invincible, and it went to my head. When she left, the last ounces of my devout holiness were snuffed out. But burning this and all other planes to the ground would never bring her back at her own volition."

I wondered how many years he'd longed for his lost love before coming to that realization. The sage wisdom of an ancient being about matters of the heart was almost humbling. No matter how long my life lasted, I could always be comforted by the risk of heartache.

"I suggest you take your new guardianship more seriously than the last I bestowed upon you," Lucifer said. "Be gone from my sight."

I blinked at him. The shadow of a smile receded from his face as he sat back down on his throne.

Ipos appeared at my side and took my hand in his, then he ushered me out of the chamber. Once in the hall, I was sucked into darkness and back to the world that felt familiar, safe, and, all of a sudden, renewed.

13
IPOS

Nestra clung to my forearm as I pulled her through the void and into her living room. The ring burned my skin, but I welcomed the painful reminder that she had made it out of Hell in one piece.

I knew what Lucifer meant when he said to take this charge more seriously. I'd been lazy in my rule over the Southwest. I'd allowed myself to indulge in mind-numbing alcohol for decades just to pass the time. Having Gaap's legions under my hand had made it easier to neglect my position and allow him to roam, going unchecked for far too long. We were not each other's keepers, but our duties and loyalties were a natural deterrent for recklessness.

With Gaap's crown fitted and his power restored, I had many choices to make. At the moment, the only one I was interested in was whether to get on my knees for Nestra and show her the gratitude that was filling my chest.

"Oh no." She snatched her hand away from my arm and looked bug-eyed at the mark her touch had left on me. "Hold on, I can heal that right up."

Before I could stop her, tell her that I was immortal and would be fine within an hour, she had bustled off to her kitchen to grab jars and balms from her cupboard. The clinking of glass followed her back with her arms full and her gaze fixed on the angry red boil on my forearm.

"Did I do this?" She sounded broken. A trip to Hell and back would do that.

"The ring did," I said, allowing her to take my injured arm in her hand.

I inhaled her scent, noting something new under the sage and rosemary. Something old and powerful was growing inside of her as she allowed her magic to flow from her diligent fingers and into the salve she used to soothe my burn. Her mortal body was caging the essence of each wound she healed, each illness she vanquished, and would hold on to it until the day she removed her enchanted gift and slipped into oblivion with me at her side.

"Nestra." I cupped my hand over hers, halting her ministrations. "Do you understand what this new life means for you? For your family?"

Her shoulders sank, and a tear fell down her flushed cheek. "I have to leave them behind."

"Not for a while, but eventually, they will wonder why you haven't aged. People who know you now will perish and leave your existence lonelier than you've ever felt, even in your worst dreams."

It was a dire warning, but necessary.

"You won't," she squeaked.

Her glassy eyes met mine and my chest constricted. "Never."

A promise I knew I could keep. Being bound to her for centuries or millennia wouldn't be long enough. I brought her hand up to my lips to kiss her knuckles.

"What now?" she asked.

The wave of reality was washing over her, and the implications of her abilities and conditional immortality were being pushed aside to focus on everyday matters.

"You patch me up and go to work."

She beamed up at me through her thick, black lashes and let one last tear roam down to her chin before bounding off her bedroom. When she came back, she held out a hand for me to take. I looked down at the ring, and she quickly adjusted her purse and belongings to her other shoulder to offer me safety.

"Let's go to work, guardian."

14

NESTRA

Introducing my family to Ipos was going to be tricky. A tall, muscular, long-haired hippie surfer who also happened to be a prince of Hell? Not exactly their idea of my perfect match.

Papa watched him over the linen draped table at the restaurant I'd chosen to meet at. I'd had to pick somewhere I knew they wouldn't make a scene. The bistro in downtown San Francisco was busy with the Saturday brunch crowd, but it was silent at our table.

The waiter came by for the fourth time to take our order, but Nico cleared his throat and said, "Another ten minutes, please."

The waiter refrained from his rolling eyes for long enough to round our table and move on to his next one.

Then Papa finally spoke. "Married. You got married without our approval?"

I had lied and said that Ipos and I ran off to Vegas to elope. Time passed differently in Hell, as I'd come to find out when we got back a whole day after Nico had come to my house. Explaining it to the police officer at my shop was less traumatic than sitting under my parents' scornful gazes in the posh restaurant.

It wasn't all a lie. To cover up our story, Ipos and I did get married in Vegas—as much as you could to a demon with a sketchy ID. The wedding photos and marriage license were real though. I hadn't shown those to Ma yet, but I had plenty of smelling salts to revive her when I did.

"*Mi amor*, why?" Ma choked into her too-white napkin.

I managed only four words of the rehearsed speech I had prepared: "It was an impulse."

"If you're feeling impulsive, you take a vacation or go to a movie," Nico scolded, sending heat up my neck. "You don't get married to a stranger you met at a bar."

Ipos' leg twitched against mine under the table. I could feel his anger through his skin and knew that he was biting for a word in the conversation.

I put my hand on Ipos' knee in solidarity. "I know this isn't the way you wanted me to find someone to spend my life with, but Poe makes me feel safe, wanted, and strong."

"What about love? Stability?" Papa chimed in, his anger abrasive over my sensitive ego. "What about the things that make a marriage real?"

"I can provide those things to your daughter, sir." Ipos spoke for the first time, and the low timbre of his voice sent a shiver down my spine, straightening it.

Papa rubbed the stubble of his chin and bore daggers into my new husband. I couldn't tell if Papa was attempting to manifest a meteor hitting only the man next to me or whether he was considering what Ipos had promised.

Though Ipos had been living in a rusty trailer in New Mexico for longer than I had been alive, he owned a distillery, many acres of property, and, apparently, a few hundred head of cattle. To say he was loaded was an understatement. He could take care of me financially for a hundred lifetimes . . . which I guessed was a real possibility now.

"*Mija*, is this man truly what your heart wants?" Ma's eyes watered, but her voice was solid. It was the matriarchal solidarity that I'd known my whole life but never really appreciated until now.

I knew that if I said I didn't want to be married anymore, they would do everything in their power to help me get the marriage to Ipos annulled. And maybe it would have been easier for me to do that while they were alive. I could have pretended to find another man, settle down, fake infertility until everyone around me withered into their mortal graves, but no. I wanted Ipos by my side for every first in my new life. I wanted to be able to lean on him openly and without shame when I needed comfort for what was going to be years of difficult decisions.

"He is perfect for me, Ma." I smiled up at my new husband.

And right on cue, he kissed my brow and whispered over my skin, "You are perfect, little witch."

I didn't care if he was lying. My heart burst, and I turned my lips up to meet his in a soft, respectful-of-my-parents kiss.

Maybe I did, or maybe I was too full of appreciation for the sacrifices he was making for me. Either way, I saw Papa's shoulders slump in defeat, then Nico sat back in his chair with a huff that said he was done fighting.

By the end of our meal, Papa and Ipos had talked about the ranch Ipos owned. They talked about land surveying, crop rotations, and, oddly enough, parasailing. It was news to all of us at the table that Papa had taken up the sport and invited Ipos out to the bay sometime for a lesson.

On our way out to our cars, Nico pulled me aside. Ipos eyed him but waited, leaning against the driver's-side door when I signaled with a nod that I was fine.

"I don't like him," Nico started, darting a look over his shoulder but not daring to linger, "but I've never seen you happier."

"I am happy," I admitted.

"If he ever gives you a hard time though—"

"You'll what?" I laughed and slapped my brother's chest and gave him a playful shove.

"I'll let Papa drown him on the parasail." His empty threat was laced with a scoff.

"I'll keep that in mind." I flung my arms around his torso, and he wrapped his around my shoulders.

"Why do I feel like I'm saying goodbye? You're going to be at the house in a couple hours for dinner."

Because he was saying goodbye to the sister he had known all his life without even realizing it. I would walk this plane healing people long after he'd retired from medicine. He wasn't losing me, but he was meeting someone I had always kept buried and hidden away beneath a shell of doubt. I had been unearthed and made into someone more powerful than he could imagine.

15

IPOS

I brought the last box of my belongings into the living room of Nestra's house. Lore greeted me with a purr and wound around my legs. The little familiar was always trying to win my favor, catch me off guard, then cause me to fall on my ass.

"Perfect timing," Nestra called from the kitchen, "dinner is almost ready."

She'd taken to our marital arrangement easier than I expected. When I'd proposed the agreement to her, I thought she would push back or find another way to explain my constant existence in her life. It wasn't until I was standing with her at the small marriage stand in Vegas that I realized how right it felt to be bound to her for all eternity. Marriage was a mortal concept. Commitment and loyalty were rarely given to the Fallen during the lifetimes we were gifted, so promising to protect and guide her until our dying days became more of a challenge and adventure than a burden.

I followed the smell of arroz con pollo and wrapped my arms around her waist. Her body melted into mine. After hours of packing and moving boxes, I realized it had been too long since we'd touched. I kissed the nape of her neck and the top of her shoulder, bringing me a pleasurable hum in response.

"Something smells delicious." I groaned into her ear. Her ass moved over my hardening cock, and I pulled her closer. "Don't start unless I can have you as my appetizer."

She arched her back and let out a mischievous giggle, knowing that her ass was grinding over my hardened length.

I dipped my hands into her loose linen shorts and found her bare for me. My head fell back, and I cursed her for enticing me on an empty stomach.

"Ten more minutes. Then we can eat and unpack." Her words were almost sing-song.

"How do you expect me to work in these conditions?" I gripped her thighs, encouraging her to spread them for me. "Can't you feel how desperate I am for a break?"

The knot of her ponytail pressed into my shoulder when she craned her head to meet my eyes. "I intend to make you beg."

That was the last straw.

I hauled her from her spot, tugged her shorts to her knees, then laid her on the kitchen table. She squealed and hollered my name as I got to my knees and gave her an eager swipe of my tongue through her wet slit.

"Oh fuck yes." She laced her fingers through my hair, letting out a moan that was enough for me to sink into her. Then, I swept my tongue over her clit and took it between my teeth to tease, bite, and roll.

"Do I still need to beg?"

"No." Her chest rose and fell with a quick suck of my lips.

"Whose pussy is this?" I demanded.

"Yours." She breathed heavily, pulling my face harder against her.

I slipped two fingers inside her cunt and was welcomed by her constricting walls. "Tell me again," I said between long strokes of my tongue.

"It's your pussy, Ipos." She edged closer, biting down on her bottom lip. She was already so close to coming undone for me.

"That's right, little witch." I removed my fingers and pulled away to sit on my heels. She looked down, confused. Frustration bloomed over her cheeks. "One."

"Ipos?" She squirmed up to sit.

"Two."

"Oh fuck." She got to her feet and discarded the shorts hanging from her ankle over her shoes.

"If I catch you . . . I fuck my little witch."

She took off through the kitchen and headed to the back door. It slammed behind her.

The hunt was on.

"Three."

I turned the stove off as I stalked by it and opened the door to find her several yards away already. Grinning to myself, I sprinted after her.

"Ipos!" she shouted, the playfulness in her voice stroking my heart. "It's still daylight."

"The whole world can watch me take what's mine over and over until the sun burns out." I caught her by the wrist.

She let out a yelp, but my mouth feasted on it until only her muffled moans could be heard as I plunged my throbbing cock inside her. I felt her heart racing and her climax rising.

"You." Thrust. "Are." Thrust. "Mine."

"Oh fuck!" She screamed through her release and clenched her thighs around my waist.

Her nails dug into my back. My name being breathlessly chanted from her lips brought me spilling inside her with a roar.

She was mine. And she would always be my most prized possession.

THE END

Thank you for coming along on Nestra and Ipos' journey. The Seven Deadly Sins series continues with Prince Of Gluttony. Join Orobas and Miss Amber for a spicy BDSM infused romance that will have you begging for more…

Choke on my Coconut

1 oz Coconut Rum

2 oz Mango Juice

1 oz Prickly Pear Vodka

1 oz Passion Fruit Liqueur

Garnish with Dragon Fruit

Acknowledgments

This year has been full of the highest highs and the lowest lows but I have been so lucky to have fierce friends by my side for the ride.

Megan, Logan, and Jess. Fuck. I love you all so much.Thank you to my chaotic Tiktok crew for being around when I needed some people to chit chat with when I should have been writing.

Shout out to my Patreon members Brandy, Logan, Megan, and Amanda!!

Thank you Cass Chapman for being a shoulder and ear.

And of course, to my bookish wifey. A. K. Mulford, you are my rock. This year wouldn't be possible without you. I love you so much.

Made in the USA
Columbia, SC
28 September 2024

43145679R00095